A dangerous stranger . . .

Clay drew one hand out of his pocket and took Jessica's. He lifted it to his lips and gently kissed it.

Jessica's pulse pounded in her ears. She prayed Clay couldn't hear it. Slowly she pulled her hand away and looked into his eyes. "Anything else?" she asked coolly. Far more coolly than she felt.

He gestured toward the bench. "Talk to me," he said softly.

"OK." Jessica felt his hand press delicately against the small of her tingling back. She let him lead her to the bench, where she sat down and slowly crossed her legs. She smiled and looked him over, her heart hammering in her chest like it hadn't in ages. The thought made her start. How long had it been? Ever since she'd first met Nick?

It was true, Jessica realized. Since Nick had come into her life, no one else had made her blood boil like the stranger sitting next to her. What did it mean? Was it what she really wanted?

"Want to know something?" Clay asked, moving closer to her.

"What?" Jessica murmured, shivering as if he'd just blown into her ear. There was something—well, a little *twisted* about this guy. What it was, she wasn't exactly sure. But she definitely didn't want to tear herself away anytime soon.

"You haven't told me your name."

Bantam Books in the Sweet Valley University series.
Ask your bookseller for the books you have missed.

Visit the Official Sweet Valley Web Site on the Internet at:

http://www.sweetvalley.com

SWEET VALLEY UNIVERSITY®

Sneaking In

**Written by
Laurie John**

**Created by
FRANCINE PASCAL**

BANTAM BOOKS
NEW YORK · TORONTO · LONDON · SYDNEY · AUCKLAND

To Kacey Michelle Cotton

RL 8, age 14 and up

SNEAKING IN

A Bantam Book / October 1998

Sweet Valley High® and Sweet Valley University®
are registered trademarks of Francine Pascal.
Conceived by Francine Pascal.
Produced by 17th Street Productions,
a division of Daniel Weiss Associates, Inc.
33 West 17th Street
New York, NY 10011.

ISBN: 0-553-57030-7

Published simultaneously in the United States and Canada

Bantam Books are published by Bantam Books, a division of Bantam
Doubleday Dell Publishing Group, Inc. Its trademark, consisting of the
words "Bantam Books" and the portrayal of a rooster, is Registered in
U.S. Patent and Trademark Office and in other countries. Marca
Registrada. Bantam Books, 1540 Broadway, New York, New York 10036.

PRINTED IN THE UNITED STATES OF AMERICA

OPM   0 9 8 7 6 5 4 3 2 1

Chapter One

"Go ahead and turn yourself into a geek, Nick Fox," Jessica Wakefield muttered under her breath. "I'm not going to be around to watch you ruin your life."

A freak morning fog was just beginning to lift off the Sweet Valley University campus. Jessica shivered as she trudged up the front steps of Denton Hall, where her nine A.M. philosophy class was due to begin in ten minutes. Once inside, she slipped quietly into the nearly empty lecture hall and took a shadowy seat in the back.

Early, Jessica thought with a cranky sigh. *I am actually early for this pointless class. I should be back in my dorm room catching up on sleep and fixing this irritating broken nail.*

Jessica stared down at the gaping chip in her otherwise glossy row of deep red nails, remembering her frustrating conversation with her boyfriend the night before.

1

"Come on," Nick had urged her, his jade green eyes glittering with excitement. "Let me sit in on a few of your classes. I'll probably be in college next semester."

"So?" Jessica had replied.

"I need a feel for what it's really like," he'd said. "I just want to see if I can hack it."

Jessica tapped her never-used pen against the writing arm of her seat. She pictured her boyfriend's sexy, crooked smile and dark tousled hair—and a panicky horror rose inside her. She still couldn't believe Nick had actually taken a leave of absence from the police force.

Jessica sighed. While every other woman on campus dated a boring college guy, she'd had a gorgeous, danger-loving undercover detective all to herself. And now what? Was her boyfriend going to turn into just another guy in a roomful of nerdy overachievers? Would impulsive, quick-tempered Nick actually raise his hand and wait for a professor to call on him? Sheesh!

What does Nick see in college anyway? Jessica fumed. One of the reasons Jessica found her boyfriend so exciting was that he *wasn't* part of the study grind scene! Nick Fox was hardly the type of guy who got off on highlighter pens and study breaks in the student union. He was a big, broad-shouldered guy who packed a .38 under his leather jacket. He worked the streets, nabbing armed robbers, murderers, and thieves. *That* was the Nick Fox she'd fallen in love with!

But now he'd gotten the noble idea to become

an attorney, just like her big brother, Steven, and her father too. Jessica didn't think Nick knew what he was getting into—four dreary years of college and three years of law school. *Blech.* But last night Nick had kept insisting he wanted to make something of himself.

"You *have* made something of yourself," Jessica had told him.

"It's not enough," Nick had pleaded. "I need to get a feel for the routine."

Routine. Ugh, Jessica thought, lifting her eyes only briefly to check out the eager-beaver students piling into the lecture hall.

She hunkered down in her seat and flipped open her empty notebook. Thank goodness Nick would never find her here. Last night he'd actually asked for her class schedule so he could tag along with her. How totally embarrassing! Of course she'd refused to give it to him. The last thing she needed was another superachiever in her life. Her twin sister, Elizabeth, was bad enough.

Jessica stared ahead numbly as Professor Malika walked into the classroom and thumped his briefcase down on the table next to the lectern.

"Hey," a deep voice murmured into her ear.

Jessica froze. She detected the familiar smell of Nick's aftershave.

"Didn't think I could track you down, did you?"

Jessica turned, dread coursing through her veins. It *was* Nick, right there in the next seat.

How could he do this to her?

3

Nick waved a hand over her eyes. "Snap out of it, Jess. It's really me."

She stared in shock at Nick's first-day-of-school outfit. Instead of his usual leather jacket and jeans he was wearing new khakis, a powder blue oxford, and glaring new running shoes. Even his unruly dark hair had been neatly combed.

The geek transformation had already begun.

"I love it when you're glad to see me," Nick whispered, reaching over and patting her leg. His powerful shoulder muscles bulged beneath his preppy shirt.

Jessica's heart sank. Nick was actually going to sit still for an entire hour and listen to dippy Professor Malika. Nick Fox—captive of Philosophy 201. It was too much to take.

She felt her face grow warm. "How did you find me?"

"I have my methods."

Jessica flipped back her long blond hair and re-settled herself in her chair. "Yes, well, why don't you just trot on down to the station and get your old job back, then?"

Nick leaned back and crossed his legs. "Aw, Jess. Come on. This'll be fun."

Jessica glared at him again, then turned hotly away.

At the front of the room Professor Malika pulled a ratty notebook out of his briefcase. After clearing his throat loudly, he grasped each side of the lectern and scowled at the assembled students. "Trust thyself," he said in a booming voice.

4

A heavy silence descended upon the room.

"Can anyone tell me which American philosopher used this phrase as his motto?" the professor demanded.

Jessica slammed her notebook shut and began doodling on its pink cover. A tiny flicker of hope began to grow inside her. Maybe it was *good* that Nick was here. After getting this taste of true boredom, it'd take wild horses to drag him back for more.

"Ralph Waldo Emerson," a young woman in the front row spoke up. "The father of the transcendentalists."

"Correct, Miss Arrington," Professor Malika said crisply. "Emerson, who dared to say the unthinkable in 1836: Man should disregard the authority of the church and society—and rely instead on his direct experience to guide his life."

"Whatever." Jessica slumped down and ran her gaze up Nick's sleeve until it finally rested on his smooth, strong profile.

Jessica's eyes widened. Nick actually looked *fascinated*. How could he think this stuff was interesting?

"But everyone's life experience is different," someone else spoke up.

Professor Malika nodded. "Though the patterns in nature are the same for everyone to see, Mr. Sikes."

"That's true, but that's not the point."

Jessica's jaw dropped as Nick's words echoed through the lecture hall. She turned her head slowly and stared in amazement. Nick was actually

5

participating in class! On his very first day! He wasn't even a *student!*

Professor Malika looked at Nick with interest. "Yes—uh—Mr. . . . ?"

"Fox," Nick said confidently. "Nick Fox."

"Go ahead, Mr. Fox."

The entire class turned to face Nick. Jessica hunched over and covered her face with her hand.

"Two different people can interpret nature differently," Nick argued calmly in his deep, sure voice. "Take a human face. One might see the face of a saint, while another might see a serial killer."

Professor Malika pointed toward Nick and nodded. "You are correct. However, the transcendentalists would not have looked into the human face for guidance. They looked to nature. To the symmetry of a leaf. The regularity of the seasons. The rebirth of life in the spring."

Nick leaned back in his seat and nodded thoughtfully.

Jessica ground her teeth. What was Nick *thinking?* Professor Malika was a jerk! He was always making up dumb philosophical questions so he could toy with his students' minds. Couldn't Nick see through that?

Nick leaned over to whisper in Jessica's ear. "This class is really interesting. Why didn't you ever tell me about it?"

"Because it's a *bore,*" Jessica hissed.

Nick turned away, distracted by a fiery debate that had erupted in the front of the room.

Jessica sighed. Was this the same Nick Fox who'd taken more than one bullet in the line of duty? The same Nick Fox who strapped a handgun to his leg for extra protection? The same Nick Fox who had once trusted *her* as his partner in undercover crime solving?

Nick Fox was the only person on earth who could help Jessica escape her boring life. And now he was completely betraying her.

She was doomed.

Little paper palm trees swung from the ceiling of the SVU dining hall. Polynesian music poured from the scratchy sound system. Tiny flowered parasols dotted tiki glasses of fruit punch.

"Pineapple pizza," Tom Watts said with a cheerful shrug as he sat down at a secluded table.

Elizabeth Wakefield took a seat beside him. "I've got the fruit salad in a mango boat."

Tom shook his head. "What's this about?"

"It's Festival Week," Elizabeth explained. "The International Student Association puts it on. You know, folk dancing in the quad, speakers on world peace. It's a South Seas theme today. Tomorrow it'll be Japanese, I think."

Elizabeth tried to take a bite of her fruit salad. Her eyes met Tom's, and they both burst out laughing.

"Octopus," Elizabeth deadpanned.

Tom raised his eyebrows. "Fish eggs."

Elizabeth covered her face with a napkin, unable to stop laughing.

"Talk about PR." Tom choked out his words. "They must be desperate to keep our spirits up."

Elizabeth felt more laughter bubbling up inside her. Not that it really had anything to do with Festival Week. It was just that she was so happy. It didn't matter where she and Tom were—the dining hall was just as good as an expensive, candlelit restaurant in Elizabeth's eyes. Her reunion with Tom had turned everything around her into a blur. They were in their own private, perfect world again. And Elizabeth loved it.

She sighed and drank in the sight of Tom. *It's amazing,* she mused, *how you can really see a person clearly after a long absence.* She took in his thick dark hair and melting brown eyes that turned up at the corners when he smiled at her.

Even the little details made her heart swell with affection. Take his denim shirt, for instance. She loved its slightly frayed collar. And the chest pocket: It was always bulging with something—reporters' notebooks, spare audiotapes, pens.

"Hmmm. Maybe I should prepare a piece on Festival Week for tonight's broadcast." Tom took a huge bite out of his pizza and smiled as he chewed.

"Why should you? You're a *serious* journalist, re-member?" Elizabeth kidded. She nudged his knee under the table and giggled. It felt so good to be able to make light of the horrible arguments they'd had during their breakup. All that I'm-a-better-reporter-than-you grandstanding was over forever. She drifted off for a moment, recalling how much had happened since that first day when she walked into the campus television studio, WSVU, to begin assisting the news desk.

Tom was already a seasoned broadcast journalist. But after only a few weeks Elizabeth was working with him on a string of hot investigative stories. At first they had been only friends. But before long the two had fallen deeply in love. When Tom had told her about the tragic car crash that had killed his entire family during his freshman year at SVU, it had brought them even closer together. Elizabeth had become all the family Tom had—or needed.

That was before George Conroy, Tom Watts's long-lost biological father, stepped into the picture. Elizabeth was happy to reunite them. But after Mr. Conroy made a series of sleazy advances toward her, Tom had refused to believe her. Her heart had been broken; her trust, shattered. She and Tom broke up for what seemed like years—long, slow, painful years.

Elizabeth left WSVU to work for the campus newspaper, the *Sweet Valley Gazette*. Before long Tom was dating a sexy, talented cellist named Dana Upshaw; Elizabeth began seeing ambitious, handsome Scott Sinclair, a fellow *Gazette* reporter. Both Dana and Scott turned out to be far less perfect than they had seemed. . . .

Tom touched her hand. "What are you thinking about?" he asked gently.

Elizabeth looked up and took a deep breath. "I was thinking . . . about how I almost lost you."

Tom's fork hung in midair. For a split second

Elizabeth thought she saw a tear in the corner of one eye, but it faded as his other hand rose up and cradled her cheek. "That's all behind us now."

Elizabeth bit her bottom lip, smiled, and nodded. For a moment she was too filled with joy to even speak.

He looked into her eyes. "Do you think I could ever let you go again?"

Elizabeth nestled her cheek in his hand, remembering how close she had come to leaving Tom—and Sweet Valley—forever. Just a couple of weeks ago she and Scott Sinclair had been on their way to the prestigious Denver Center for Investigative Reporting. She and Scott had actually boarded their plane for Denver when Tom ran on board, told Elizabeth he loved her, and took her off the airplane in his arms.

Elizabeth sighed. Even the horrible things Scott had said to her that day couldn't take away the bliss she felt when she saw Tom's face and heard his loving words.

She stirred her drink with a straw, remembering with sudden clarity the urgency and passion of Tom's kiss in that airport terminal. Still, she knew now that the moment wasn't just about a kiss. And it wasn't even just about Tom. It was a moment when a door seemed to open for her. A moment when all the confusion and uncertainty in her life seemed to melt away.

She knew then, in her own heart, that she loved Tom. That she needed to stay at SVU. And that she didn't want to live so far away from her twin sister,

Jessica. The dream of leaving for DCIR hadn't been her own dream. It had been Scott's.

"I guess you should be mad at me for keeping you from one of the top journalism schools in the country," Tom teased.

"SVU is just as good," Elizabeth defended. "Besides, DCIR isn't about to close down or anything. Maybe I'll go there for grad school."

"Well, in the meantime," Tom began, "how'd you like to come back to WSVU? This campus is full of stories just waiting for us to pounce on together. Just think of what we could expose, like those outrageously highly paid computer science profs. Who's paying them off anyway?"

Elizabeth smiled.

"And what about these guys?" Tom nodded sideways toward the kitchen. "I've heard they've been cited for poor food-handling practices. . . ."

Elizabeth stopped chewing and stared down at her fruit salad. "Your wanting me to come back to WSVU wouldn't have anything to do with the amount of time we'd be spending together, would it?" She looked up and gazed into his serious brown eyes. "Or do you really want to straighten out the world that much?"

Tom's expression softened. "Guess which."

Elizabeth could have taken his face in her hands and kissed him right then. Still, she knew herself well enough not to let a guy—no matter how wonderful a guy—affect an important decision about her work as a journalist.

She winced slightly. She couldn't forget how she'd let Scott talk her into leaving WSVU for a reporting job at the *Gazette*. Of course, that had been *before* she and Scott became involved, and print journalism had always been her first love. But she'd made the move *after* the breakup with Tom.

Would she have done the same thing if she and Tom had been together? Probably not. That didn't mean she'd made a bad decision. And that didn't mean she had to return now that they were a couple again. . . .

"Please come back to WSVU," Tom whispered. He leaned forward on his elbows, his eyes pleading.

"I can't," Elizabeth heard herself say. "Not right now."

Tom fell back in his chair and looked up at the ceiling. "Why not?"

"Because I love what I'm doing at the *Gazette*."

"What can you do at the *Gazette* that you can't do even better with me at WSVU?" Tom argued. "It's not just words you have to work with in TV. We've got visuals. Emotion. Action."

Elizabeth straightened. "And only a few minutes to get your message across."

Tom opened his mouth to speak, then closed it and looked down at his fists.

"I like print too much to give it up," Elizabeth said simply. "Take everything I did for WSVU and multiply it by ten—*that's* what I put into each piece I write for the *Gazette*. Research. Insight. Impact. You name it. The printed word is so much more . . . *powerful*."

Elizabeth watched as Tom tightened his fist. He finally loosened it and took a deep breath. "OK," he whispered. "I'm not going to push it. You know what you're doing."

"Yes."

Tom smiled.

Elizabeth felt a pang. "And maybe . . ." She shook her head. "No."

Tom arched his eyebrows. "What?"

Sighing, Elizabeth arranged her thoughts into words. "Maybe I don't want anything to—to jeopardize what we have," she explained. "I want to take things slow and easy. If I'm working with you every day, there's just no breathing room for us."

"Breathing room?" The corners of Tom's eyes seemed to fall.

Elizabeth gave him a gentle kick under the table. "You know what it was like. When we were working at WSVU, we were together every second. I want things to be different this time."

A long silence fell between them. Elizabeth tried not to hear the tacky hula music and boisterous laughter around her. She knew Tom had been hurt by her decision, but she knew she'd made the right one—for herself.

Tom cleared his throat. He took his denim jacket from the back of his chair and dug into a side pocket. "I kind of figured you wouldn't change your mind."

Elizabeth raised her eyebrows. "You did?"

"Yeah," he whispered, setting a small, carefully

13

wrapped gift on the table between them. "So this . . . this is for you."

They leaned back and shared a smile. Elizabeth suddenly felt shy and secure at the same time.

"Sorry I've been a jerk," Tom apologized.

Elizabeth picked up the gift gingerly and shook it next to her ear. "Not a jerk. Just . . . domineering."

"But I didn't persuade you."

"Nope." Elizabeth slipped off the gold ribbon and pulled the paper off a narrow silver box. Slowly she lifted the top. Inside, a beautiful gold fountain pen lay on a bed of pure white cotton. The pen was inlaid with intricate patterns of mother-of-pearl. "Where did you ever—?"

"It was my mother's," Tom said quietly.

"Oh, Tom . . ."

"She would have wanted you to have it," Tom whispered, his voice catching. "If she'd had the chance to meet you."

Elizabeth shook her head wordlessly. It always had been hard for Tom to talk about his mother, but this one simple gesture told her everything.

"Thank you," Elizabeth said, her eyes filling with tears. "Thank you so much, Tom."

Tom shrugged. "You're a writer at heart, Elizabeth. I guess I've finally figured that out. And every good writer like you should have a good pen."

Elizabeth smiled. "Maybe you're right."

"We'll take things one step at a time, huh?" Tom squeezed her hand. "And if you someday decide to come back to WSVU, you've got your old job waiting for you."

She lifted up his hand and kissed it. Nothing, *nothing* could ever make her leave him again.

"Here's your change!" Isabella Ricci handed a group of students a shopping bag stuffed with three Hug the World T-shirts. "Wash them in cold water!"

The quad's long, carefully manicured stretch of grass and trees had been taken over by rows of festive booths all trying to lure the throngs of students emerging from the Wednesday afternoon science labs and literature seminars. The SVU World Peace Club featured a Jamaican steel drum band performing on a raised wooden platform. The Save Our Planet Alliance ran a video describing devastation in the Amazon rain forest. And each of SVU's sororities and fraternities sold their own special T-shirts and information on recycling, studying abroad, and volunteering.

"Whew," Isabella sighed. She sat down on a tiny stool behind the Theta Alpha Theta booth and opened the cash box. "That's twenty T-shirts in the last hour alone. At this rate the campus is going to be drowning in that slogan."

"I like the design, though," Denise Waters said. She ran her fingers through her silky brunette bob and fanned her face in the heat. "It's cute and colorful."

"And the Thetas get to help raise the level of world consciousness," Isabella joked.

"Just one of our many talents," Denise said with a giggle. She skipped over to the cooler at the back of the booth. "I brought some bottles of iced coffee for us. Thought it would keep us awake during booth duty."

"What are you talking about?" Isabella argued, squirting sunblock onto her porcelain-pale shoulders and rubbing it in. Her long jet-black hair curled down her back. "Everyone's here. I'm having a totally great time."

Denise nodded. "Maybe you're right. It's better than studying, that's for sure."

"Hey!" Isabella called over to the Sigmas in the adjoining booth. "Not much action over there this afternoon? Lost your golden touch?"

"We'd sell more Whirled Peas hats if you'd model one for us, Isabella," Sigma treasurer James Montgomery kidded. He patted his knee. "Come on over here."

Isabella laughed. "Forget it!"

"Heartbreaker!" James teased back.

Isabella caught a glimpse of Todd Wilkins emerging from one of the academic buildings. He hoisted his backpack and squinted into the sun. "Todd!" she yelled across the crowd. "Want to buy a T-shirt?"

Todd approached the Theta booth and wiped his forehead with his wrist. "Are the Thetas selling anything to drink? I'm dying of thirst."

"Nope," Isabella said with a grin. She grabbed an ice-cold Coke from the cooler. "But I'll give it to you for free."

"Thanks." Todd opened the soda and took a swig. "What's up?"

Isabella put her hands on her hips. "Selling T-shirts to help save the world for future generations."

"Save the world?" Todd chuckled. "Yeah, right. You're just trying to draw some new Theta recruits."

"No way," James chimed in. "The Thetas are looking for aggressive, warrior women. They're not the peace-loving type."

"You guys are awful," Denise protested.

"Working hard, ladies?"

Isabella's stomach turned at the sound of the whiny voice. Sure enough, Theta vice president Alison Quinn was weaving her way through the crowd and making a beeline for the booth.

"See you 'ladies' later." Todd rolled his eyes. "Looks like someone's here to check up on you."

"Oooh. Gee. I'll be back in a sec," Denise said suddenly. "I need to grab some of that free pineapple pizza from the food service booth."

"Hey—," Isabella began, but Denise was gone in a flash. Isabella made a face and leaned on the booth's counter. *Wouldn't you know it,* she thought with a groan. *Just when things get fun, the Wicked Witch in the Wonderbra shows up.*

Alison turned to watch Denise retreat into the crowd. "Gone so soon?" she asked snidely. She flipped up the hinged section of the counter and ducked inside. Her stern gray eyes quickly took in the state of the sorority's booth. Immediately she began tidying the stacks of T-shirts.

"Denise went to get a bite to eat," Isabella explained.

Alison's expression turned chilly. When she was done fussing with the T-shirts, she began counting the money in the cash box.

Isabella smiled. Alison was by far the rudest Theta in recorded history, but even *she* couldn't dampen Isabella's upbeat mood. "The T-shirts are a very hot item, Alison. We've sold thirty-five since we opened this morning."

"Mmmm." Alison ran a manicured finger over an extra box of carefully folded shirts. "Good."

"Put one on, Alison," Isabella said, holding up a size small. "White is your color. It'll show off your tan."

"You talked me into it." Alison obediently pulled the T-shirt over her own and smiled. She smoothed out her hair and gave Isabella a long stare. "So, how's Danny Wyatt these days?"

Isabella smiled weakly and looked at her watch. "He'd be right here at my side if he wasn't in the middle of an important physics exam."

Alison adjusted the yellow-and-white-striped booth awning, then wiped down the counter. "Sounds like he's pretty possessive. How can you stand it?"

Isabella sank back down on her stool and fiddled with her bracelet. "Oh, I can stand it OK. Danny's the most devoted guy I could hope for."

"Still . . . ," Alison said with a suspicious look, "I think the beautiful bird is beginning to rattle her cage."

Isabella laughed. "Don't worry about us. I'm used to Danny's insane jealousy," she said with soap opera exaggeration. "It's his way of telling me he loves me."

"Uh-huh," Alison said. "And I bet you go right along with it just to avoid hurting his feelings. You should talk to him about that."

Isabella stared at Alison in wonder. Strangely enough, her comments struck a chord. When did *Alison Quinn* turn sympathetic? Alison was the kind of person who thought the movie *Scream* was a sort of tender romance.

"I mean, Danny has to be able to trust you," Alison went on. "If you don't mind my saying so."

Isabella waved her comment away. "No, no, Alison. It's OK. I know what you're saying."

Alison crossed her arms over her chest. "What else does he do?"

"Well." Isabella bit her lip. "Just to give you a mild example, Danny insists on coming with me to my history study group. He's convinced there's a guy there who's after me."

"Is he?"

Isabella smiled. "Of course."

Alison laughed. "*You're* the one who has to draw the boundaries, Izzy. Not Danny. That's my opinion."

Isabella sighed. "I know you're right. It's just that . . ."

19

"It's easier not to take a stand, I know," Alison sympathized. "But you've got to."

Take a stand? Isabella wondered as a lively Ethiopian drum-and-song ensemble began warming up at a nearby stage. *With Danny? I'm not sure—*

"Hey, anyone care to dance?"

Isabella shook herself out of her minitrance and glanced at the chestnut-haired guy leaning over the partition between the Theta and Sigma booths.

"Hi, Derrick," Alison said flatly. She stepped away from Isabella to help a customer.

Isabella smiled at Derrick Ecker, the cute Sigma from Seattle who played his saxophone at a lot of frat parties. "Helping the Sigmas save the world?" she asked politely.

"Yep." Derrick grinned. He suddenly leaned forward and looked right at her.

Isabella rolled her eyes.

"May I ask you something, Isabella?"

Isabella put her hands on her hips and looked back at him matter-of-factly. Derrick's face was inches from hers. She was amazed she'd never noticed how bright and blue his eyes were, because he was always flirting with her. Then again, he was always flirting with *everybody*. "OK, Derrick. Shoot."

"Do you want to get out of here?"

Isabella laughed. "Are you kidding? I've still got another hour to put in. Besides . . ."

"Besides *what?*" Derrick taunted, pulling closer and slipping the palm of his hand up the side of her face. His fingers pulled gently through her dark, loose curls. "You've been in here forever. I've been watching you."

Isabella pressed her lips together, then burst out laughing. "Oh yeah. I bet you have, Derrick."

She shook her head. Derrick was the kind of guy who loved to imagine that women were ready to fall at his feet when he snapped his fingers. He lived in a dream world, for sure—he and most of his Sigma brothers.

"Come on, Izzy," Derrick teased.

Isabella looked right at him and struggled to keep a straight face. "Maybe you've never taken a close look at my boyfriend, Derrick. He eats guys like you for breakfast."

"Well, I hope he's treating you right, because you're the most beautiful creature I've ever seen."

"Uh-huh." Isabella crossed her arms over her chest. "And where's Debbie?"

Derrick's eyebrows knitted together. "Who's Debbie?"

"Um, your *girlfriend?*" Isabella giggled. "The one you gave that beautiful engraved locket to last weekend? She showed it to me. Sounds serious."

"Mmmm," Derrick murmured, staring at the lock of her hair in his hand. "You've got a point there."

Isabella threw a look over her shoulder. Alison was busy helping a line of customers and wasn't likely to rescue her from Derrick's teasing anytime soon. She glanced past Derrick and saw that several of his Sigma brothers were staring at them.

21

OK, game over, Isabella thought impatiently. She had been a Theta long enough to know that innocent flirting with the Sigmas was a part of everyday sorority life, but this was going too far. She backed away, but the Sigma ring on Derrick's finger had become entangled in her hair. Suddenly her head jerked toward his.

Chapter Two

"Jessica! Wait up!" Nick called out above the thundering sound of a hundred students pouring out of the lecture hall at once. Professor Malika had excused the class only moments before, but Jessica had already sprung out of her seat and was now squeezing herself into the crowd at the door.

Nick shook his head. He knew what she was doing. From the moment he'd sat down next to Jessica, it was clear she didn't want him there in class with her. Speaking up in class had probably been a mistake too. She was obviously furious with him.

"Come on, Jess," Nick muttered. He pushed past a group of guys huddled around a bulletin board. "Cut it out."

He spotted Jessica's silky blond hair bobbing in the crush of backpacks and jackets. Finally he got close enough to put his hand on her shoulder. "Where are you going?"

Jessica paused for a moment before she turned to face him. "Oh. Sorry."

Nick tried to look at her sternly, but it was tough. Jessica was irresistible when she was angry. Her beautiful sea green eyes flashed. Her skin turned rosy. And her face took on that tough expression that always reminded him of how much Jessica hated not getting her way.

"That was our first class together," Nick reminded her.

"I said I was sorry," Jessica said. She turned away to push open the door.

Nick reached out and opened it for her. Jessica walked quickly outside and hurried down the flight of steps leading to the crowded quad. "What's the big deal, Jess?" he asked. He had to jog to keep up with her.

"Nothing."

Nick picked up the pace as Jessica clipped past the festive booths set up all along the main quad. "I liked your philosophy class."

"I could tell."

Nick stared at Jessica's stern profile. A breeze blew her shiny hair back off her face. He could see every inch of her smooth skin and the lush pout of her lips. He knew she wasn't just angry about how he showed up in her class. Ever since he took an absence from the police force to give college a try, she'd been furious with him. But what could he do? He had a dream, and he wanted to see it come true. The only obstacle in his path was convincing Jessica that it was the right thing.

"I think I'm going to do a little reading," Nick went on, trying to ignore Jessica's bad mood. "I mean, I want to be a lawyer, and lawyers could use a little deep thinking once in a while, don't you think?"

"Uh-huh."

"Those philosophy and literature courses really make you use your brain, don't they?"

"Sure, they do."

"Jessica?" Nick touched her shoulder as she began walking even faster.

"Yes?"

Nick skipped forward until he was in front of her. Walking backward, he tried to catch her eye. "Hey. I know what this is about. But try to understand."

Jessica brushed past him.

Nick sucked in his breath and let it out in frustration. Every reminder of his decision to change careers upset her. Even when his college entrance exams came back with high scores, she'd looked at him as if he were completely crazy.

"Tell me what's wrong," Nick said patiently.

"Nothing's wrong." Jessica pouted.

Nick smiled at her and slipped his hand in hers. "Come here. Sit down with me."

"I'm in a hurry."

Nick patiently steered her toward a bench next to the French club's croissant-and-café-au-lait booth. He had to remind himself that Jessica wasn't always what she appeared to be. Sure, her face looked tough and her words were sharp. But that was usually Jessica's way of begging for attention.

Jessica hugged her books even more tightly to her chest as she sat down. "Don't you have to be somewhere?" she asked bluntly. "Like maybe back at the precinct? On your knees? Begging for your old job back?"

Nick slipped his arm around her waist. "Come on. I'm happy with my leave of absence, and you know it. And *that* means we can have lunch together today to talk about this."

"Talk about what?" Jessica asked shortly.

"Why you're so mad, and why I'm so strangely content."

"I can't."

Nick shrugged, crossed a leg over his knee, and spread his arms out along the back of the bench. "Tell me. Does Professor Malika assign papers, or is he a strictly essay-question-exam kind of guy?"

"I don't know. I forget," Jessica said. She stared restlessly out at the passing crowd.

Nick stared. "Are you kidding? You don't know if you have a paper to write for the class?"

"Um . . . actually, I think we do."

Nick brightened. "I could help you. I'm thinking of auditing the class since I won't be starting college until next semester."

The anger in Jessica's blue-green eyes turned to panic. "But what if it's the wrong decision? What if you wake up tomorrow morning and realize it's all a big mistake?"

Nick took her face in his hands. "Then I'll get my old job back."

"You'll never do that," Jessica said abruptly. She dug into her purse and pulled out a mirror and tube of lipstick. "You're too proud."

Nick watched in frustration as she coated her lips in shiny red and snapped the tube shut. What did she expect him to do? Throw away his dreams of a college degree just because she'd had a great time helping him with a few stings? Sure, Jessica had great instincts and had been a huge help. But he had other mountains to climb now.

Jessica let out a long, bored sigh and watched the crowds move past them. She tapped her toes to the lively African music booming from the festival's central platform.

Nick took her hand and tried another approach. "Look. I know you've been through a lot lately."

Jessica gave him an impatient look. "I have?"

Nick nodded. "Things have been crazy. Just a couple of weeks ago you thought you were going to be living apart from your twin sister for the first time in your life. Then I decided to leave the force. That's a lot of trauma."

"Mm-hmm."

"I'll check with you first next time," Nick said carefully. "I mean, before I crash one of your classes."

"Thank you," Jessica said lightly. Suddenly she stood up. "Now if you don't mind, I've got an art history class to get to."

Nick held up his hands and remained on the bench. "OK, Jess. Maybe we can get together for a

27

late study break after I finish my reading. I'll call you."

"OK," Jessica said quickly before walking away.

Nick watched Jessica slip into the crowd. He shook his head. Strong-willed, passionate Jessica. He knew she was addicted to excitement, yet he also knew she needed the steady love and support only he could give her. They were going through some changes, Nick had to admit. And true to Jessica Wakefield form, she was clamming up. She always did when her feelings were confused.

What Jessica needs now, Nick told himself, *is a safe, normal relationship.* No more crazy stakeouts. No more undercover jobs, scrounging for evidence in the middle of the night among hardened criminals. It was time they settled down into the life they were meant to have: a nice, quiet routine on a college campus.

Danny Wyatt hiked his backpack up on his shoulder as he made his way out into the quad after his physics class. His eyes were blurry and his nerves shot, thanks to the killer exam he'd just taken.

Up ahead was the colorful flutter of Festival Week booths, the sounds of laughter and music. He slipped on his sunglasses and tried to shake off his prickly postexam stress.

For some weird reason his mind kept replaying a conversation he'd had with his roommate, Tom Watts, that morning. It had started out innocently while they were shaving over the sinks in the bathroom on their floor in Reid Hall. Tom had been jazzed ever since he'd gotten back together with his girlfriend, Elizabeth Wakefield—and Danny was just jazzed to see Tom happy after so many weeks of confusion and misery. Somehow the conversation got around to great women in general. Tom—being the enthusiastic guy he was—had started talking up Danny's girlfriend, Isabella Ricci.

"You're lucky to have her, man," Tom had said.

"What was that supposed to mean, Tom?" Danny muttered under his breath as he walked toward the booths. Yeah, he was lucky. Isabella was incredible. Anyone would be lucky to have Isabella. But why did Tom happen to think *Danny*, in particular, was lucky?

The path Danny took back to the dorms was usually a place of cool, serene lawns and softly rustling trees. But the scores of booths, food stands, and sound stages in his path jolted his raw nerves even further. He considered turning around and taking another route, but his thirst got the better of him.

"I'll take a Coke," Danny told the guy selling soba noodles, pad Thai, and egg rolls at the Association of Asian Students booth. He paid and took a big gulp from the plastic cup, crunching the ice between his teeth.

Admit it. You really are lucky to have Isabella for a girlfriend, a voice in Danny's head taunted. He paused to stare at the African drum-and-song performance taking place on a raised platform next to the quad's fountain. *What would most beautiful, intelligent women see in you anyway? You're no heavy-duty athlete. You can't dance. And you're probably only so-so in the romantic department.*

But Isabella loves me the way I am, Danny silently argued.

A crash of applause broke through Danny's warring thoughts. The performance had ended, and the musicians began filing off the platform.

As the applause died away, Danny's mind drifted back to last week, when he'd taken Isabella on a moonlight canoe ride on the campus lake. They'd noticed a couple in another rented canoe. They could barely make out the dim figure of a guy standing up in the boat, horsing around and tipping it back and forth. The girl with him was laughing hysterically. A few moments later came a loud splash, followed by more laughter.

Isabella had laughed too, Danny remembered. But then she had stretched back from her spot on the bow and touched his knee. "Want to know another thing I love about you?" she had asked.

"What?" he'd said, staring into Isabella's beautiful face, luminous in the moonlight.

"This may sound funny, but I love knowing that you're not going to suddenly stand up in this boat and tip it over."

Danny had nodded and leaned forward to kiss her. "You're right about that."

"I always feel like you're watching out for me, Danny," Isabella had said.

The memory reassured him. Danny suddenly felt as if he could breathe again. A feeling of well-being washed over him as he strolled past the booths, taking in the smells and sounds. Of course Isabella loved him. Of course Danny deserved her. All he had to do was think of the feel of her silky black hair in his hands, the way her gray eyes sparkled with love when she stroked the side of his face. . . .

Danny suddenly stopped in midthought. His eye was caught by three familiar Greek letters—Theta Alpha Theta—printed across a fluttering awning. He slowed and stared at two figures. A moment later he realized what he was seeing.

"Isabella?" Danny whispered. He stopped. His legs suddenly felt like two marble columns planted into the ground. He felt all the breath rush out of his body.

There, less than twenty-five yards away from him, sat Isabella, her face practically mashed into the face of a muscular-looking guy he'd never seen before in his life.

Danny couldn't move. Everything around him faded into the white-hot of his anger. The music stopped. The laughter disappeared. Even the crush of people around him froze. All he could see was Isabella's slender back and the face of the stranger who was insinuating his hands through her hair.

Then, just when he thought things couldn't get worse, he saw Isabella move suddenly toward the guy, as if she were giving him an impulsive kiss.

"Isabella!" he heard himself shout.

Danny felt his heart ripping in two. The press of the crowd seemed to swallow him up. Memories began to needle him. He flashed on all the times Isabella had told him she had to study. Each time she had been the first to pull away from a kiss. Even the excuse she'd made last night when he had asked her to drive out to the beach with him this afternoon: *I have to sell T-shirts for the Thetas.*

Of course she did, Danny thought. *Of course she did.*

Suddenly Danny felt an uncontrollable rage flowing through his veins. He stepped back, then stepped forward, and stepped again and again until he was running toward her.

"Isabella!" he shouted, shoving away a guy walking his bike.

"Watch it!" the guy yelled angrily.

"What are you doing?" Danny bellowed, though he was too far away for Isabella to hear him yet. She was still nuzzling this guy as if she'd never heard of Danny Wyatt. Right in front of everybody.

Danny crushed his paper cup in his fist and flung it down. Of course Danny was "lucky" to have Isabella. In fact, their whole relationship was too good to be true. She was proving it to him right now. But Danny wasn't about to let her humiliate him like this. And he was going to tell her so right now. Right in front of that guy. Right in front of everybody.

"I'm staying in this library for exactly ten more seconds, Nick," Jessica declared as she snapped her compact shut.

Nick held up one finger. "Just another minute, Jess," he whispered as he flipped madly through the pages of a dusty old book.

Jessica's jaw dropped. "This wasn't the plan. You said you would pick up the book and leave. I promised you exactly five minutes in this morgue."

Nick shifted in his seat. "Just give me some time, OK? I'm not sure this is the book I need."

"I haven't had dinner, and I'm starved," Jessica complained. "Three more seconds and I'm walking out."

"Uh-huh," Nick mumbled.

Jessica shook her head with exasperation. Only a few weeks ago she and Nick had been tearing about town, partners in murder investigations and under-cover operations like the Sweet Valley police force had never seen. Now they were acting like a couple of ordinary geeks.

Well, *Nick* was anyway.

Jessica dug into her bag and found a stick of gum. She folded it into her mouth as she stared at Nick.

Nick looked up. "What?"

"OK." Jessica snapped her gum and held up two fingers. "Two more minutes."

Nick drew his ballpoint pen up to his lips and bit down on it thoughtfully.

Jessica cringed. "What are you reading?"

"It's a book about the eighteenth-century crimi-nal justice system in America," Nick said. "I think I'll check it out. It's incredible."

"Fascinating."

Nick nodded absently. "It really is."

Jessica sighed and plucked a nail file from her purse.

Bo-ring.

Why in the world did she let Nick drag her down to the library? Everything about it was driving her crazy. The quiet, creepy way people slipped up and down the stacks. The dry sound of turning pages. The deadly fluorescent overhead lights, which made Nick's rugged face look pasty. She shuddered. Who knew *what* they were doing to her *own* complexion.

Worst of all, she hated how the library made her feel: bored. *Bored with Nick Fox,* Jessica thought glumly. *Who'd have thought it could happen?*

"I need to get out of here," Jessica said suddenly. She snapped her purse shut and stood up.

Nick glanced at his watch. "And *I* need a little more time."

"Enough." Jessica grabbed the book from Nick's hand and scanned the cover. "*Trends in Eighteenth-Century American Justice,* by Samuel H. Blinkenstaff?" she read. "Give me a break. Why don't you just check it out now? This place is giving me a major case of the heebie-jeebies."

Nick calmly took the book from Jessica. "OK, Jess. Five more minutes."

Jessica stood there, fuming, as Nick stuck the pen between his teeth again. Suddenly he pulled the pen out of his mouth and drew his hand up to his lips. They were dripping with dark blue ink.

"Ugh," Nick groaned. Spatters of ink stained the front of his oxford. "Jess? You have a tissue or—"

"Here," Jessica snapped. She whipped a clean tissue out of her purse and handed it to him.

"Must have bitten down too hard on that damn thing," Nick said quietly. He blotted his blue chin. "Let's take off. OK?"

Jessica cringed. Even Nick's *teeth* were stained blue. He looked like a monster. How could she be seen walking out of the library with him?

She had to face facts. Nick needed rescuing— and fast—from his experiment with geekdom. The first thing she was going to do was show him what she would and, most importantly, would *not* put up with. Wait—make that second. First she had to beat a hasty retreat.

Jessica stood up, her chair scraping loudly against the floor. She slung her purse over her shoulder. "Catch you later." She turned on her heel and marched toward the exit.

"Jess! Wait up!" Nick whispered loudly.

Yeah. Right. Like I want to be seen with you, Jessica thought as she left the stacks and pushed through the exit stiles. Outside, the evening air was cool and the long, empty quad was finally quiet. Above, the sky was studded with stars. Jessica suddenly wanted to fly up into them. Hugging her books lightly to her chest, she strolled slowly, breathing in the wet smell of freshly mowed grass.

"Nice night, huh?"

Jessica looked over in the direction of the voice. A guy was sitting all by himself on a quad bench. He had one arm sprawled along its backrest as if he too had been looking up at the night sky.

She paused and drew in her breath sharply. In the hazy light of the quad lamps she could see that this guy wasn't just anyone. He was gorgeous in an offbeat, even exotic way. She took in his shapely mouth, long brown hair, and large, melting, chocolate brown eyes. Lanky and muscular, he wore jeans, a plain black T-shirt, and a thin string of black leather around his wrist.

"Jess!" Nick bellowed.

"He's calling," the guy said softly. He gave her a soulful look before sticking his hands in his pockets and standing up. Then, before she could say a thing, he turned and strolled slowly away.

"Yes," Jessica whispered. A thrill zipped up her spine as the broad-shouldered figure disappeared into darkness.

"Why did you leave?" Nick complained as he jogged up to where she was standing. "You knew I wanted to check out the book. I need your library card."

"Sorry," Jessica said absently. Her eyes lingered on the shadowy figure.

Too delicious, she thought as the guy slipped across the grass and out of sight.

With a grunt Isabella finally managed to untangle her hair from Derrick's fraternity ring.

"Sorry," Derrick said with a grin. He twisted the chunky ring on his finger and raked back his thick hair. "You should be more careful."

Isabella gave Derrick an exasperated look and smoothed out her curls. "You totally blew that one, Mr. Don Juan. You could use some practice."

"Hey. You can't blame me for trying, can you?"

Isabella rolled her eyes. "Whatever."

"Isabella!"

Isabella smiled and turned around at the sound of Danny's voice. She shaded her eyes and searched the crowd. Why did he sound so upset? His physics exam must have been a killer.

Suddenly she saw his familiar face in the crowd—his dark cocoa skin, his angular cheek-bones. When he was just a few yards from the booth, her smile faded. Danny's eyes were flashing, and his lean jaw was tensed with anger. "Danny?" she called. "Danny, what's wrong?"

A moment later he yanked his backpack from his shoulder as if he were preparing for a fight. Sweat trickled down the side of his neck.

Isabella stepped back. "Danny! What's—"

"What the hell are you doing?" Danny threw his pack to the ground. He slammed both hands down on the counter, startling two young women buying T-shirts from Alison.

"What's wrong?" Isabella cried.

"You know what's wrong," Danny shouted. He pushed past Alison's two customers until he found the counter entrance and ducked into the booth.

Isabella stared at Danny's crazed expression. She realized it wasn't directed at her but just over her shoulder. Her heart pounding with worry, she turned to look at Derrick.

Derrick's face had paled. He held up his palms and backed away. "Hey, dude. Listen—"

"Back off!" Danny poked Derrick's chest with his index finger. "She happens to be *my* girlfriend!"

"Sure thing, pal. No problem," Derrick said quietly. He slipped out of the Sigma booth and jogged into the crowd.

"But . . . wait!" Isabella called after Derrick just before he disappeared completely into the crowd.

Danny grabbed Isabella's arm and wrenched her around. "What do you want with him?" he demanded.

"What are you talking about?" Isabella whispered.

"You were coming on to him," Danny said, his dark eyes blazing. "I could see it from halfway across campus."

Isabella flushed with anger. She shook his hand off her arm and planted her hands on her hips. "Are you kidding?"

"No, I am not kidding!"

"Well, *Derrick* was," Isabella explained. "It's an old Sigma-Theta tradition, in case you didn't know."

"Then why did you have your face planted into his?"

Isabella tried to think. "What? You mean, when he . . . Jeez, Danny. His fraternity ring got caught in my hair."

38

"That's a really creative story," Danny said, sarcasm dripping from his voice.

"Stop it, Danny! It's true!"

"Would you mind toning it down, please?" Alison whispered angrily as she slammed the cash box shut. "The Thetas are trying to make a good impression here."

Isabella whipped open a canvas flap at the back of the booth and dragged Danny out by the arm. "What do you think you're doing? Did you think I was flirting with him or something?"

"You were doing more than flirting."

"I was *not* flirting with him," Isabella said hotly.

Danny set his jaw. "His hands were all over you, and I didn't see you doing anything about it."

"You're crazy!"

"Oh, am I?" Danny cried. "No. I *was* crazy to think you were being faithful to me. Now I know what you do when I'm not around!"

"You don't understand," Isabella said, hot tears burning her eyes. "The Sigmas—they're our brother fraternity. The Sigs and Thetas are always joking around like that. It's a Greek thing."

"How cute."

Isabella groaned. "Danny, your whole jealousy thing has got to stop," she pleaded, forcing her voice to remain low. "And your attitude—it's too smothering. You're suffocating me."

"Oh yeah. Right." Danny pressed his lips together as if he were trying to contain billowing steam inside his head.

"I—I don't know what else to say," Isabella told him tearfully.

Danny didn't respond. He just shook his head, turned on his heel, and stomped off. "See you around—maybe."

Isabella stood there, her heart hammering in her chest, her mind in shock. What could Danny be thinking? After all they'd said to each other and all the love they'd shared, how could he possibly think she was interested in any guy but him? The whole idea was ludicrous.

Brushing away tears, Isabella slipped back into the Theta booth and quickly took her place behind the counter, where four new customers were lined up, eagerly waving bills at Alison.

"Where have you been?" Alison whispered angrily.

Isabella bit her bottom lip. "I—I guess I'm just having some problems—"

"Well, they've got to stop," Alison hissed.

"Wha . . . ?"

Alison's face was livid. "You are a Theta, Isabella. You represent this organization. Your behavior today reflects badly on all of us."

Isabella wiped a tear. "I'm so sorry—"

"You signed up to work this booth until five," Alison snapped. "I would appreciate it if you wouldn't abandon your job until your time is up."

"OK."

"And don't think I won't report this to the Theta board, Isabella. You've disgraced us!"

Chapter Three

Nick, you are a real heartbreaker, Jessica fumed. She pushed through the entrance to Dickenson Hall and stormed inside.

Jessica marched through the first-floor lounge, which was crammed with UNICEF posters and information tables on exchange student programs. Two girls were sprawled on the floor, laughing and picking on their acoustic guitars.

Eyes filling with tears, she hurried to the staircase, taking the steps two at a time. Once she reached the second floor, she breathed in the familiar dorm smell of shampoo, microwaved popcorn, and new carpeting. Somehow it made her feel worse than ever.

She'd left Nick in front of the library. He'd been irritating her with stupid questions, like why she didn't have a library card. Jessica shuddered just picturing the way he kept dabbing his ink-stained teeth with tissue. Of course she didn't give him a good-night kiss. Puh-*leeze!*

But now that she was back in her boring dorm, Jessica knew she'd made a mistake. What she needed was a large party. Or a late night shopping trip to the mall. Definitely *not* the dorm. She needed to shake off her frustration somehow.

What am I supposed to do, Nick? Just sit there and watch you turn yourself into someone you're not supposed to be?

"You have let me down, Nick. You have committed *fraud*," Jessica whispered to herself when she reached the door to room 28. "It's called false advertising. And if you don't do something about it, I'm going to take you to court!"

"Hi, Jess! How come you're talking to your door?"

Jessica stretched a bright smile across her face. The hallway had been blissfully empty, but now the nosy music major neighbor known to Jessica as "Trumpethead" had suddenly materialized as if from thin air. "I'm practicing my lines for a big audition," Jessica lied.

"Oh. Cool!" Trumpethead said brightly. She headed toward the shower room with a towel over her arm.

Jessica burned inside. There was no way she was going to let anyone in the dorm know that her romance with Nick Fox could possibly be in trouble. She and Nick were practically dorm legend. They were above gossip and speculation. With an exasperated sigh she flung open the door and slammed it shut.

"What's wrong?" Elizabeth asked.

Jessica stared. Elizabeth was a picture of level-headed calm. She was sitting cross-legged on her bed, sewing a flowered patch onto an old pair of jeans. Her blond hair was pulled back into a shiny ponytail, and her perfectly smooth skin had an especially rosy cast.

"Something happen between you and Nick?" Elizabeth asked innocently.

Jessica stiffened. "It's ten-fifteen on a week-night, and you're not studying?"

Elizabeth looked down, completely unruffled, and made another tiny stitch. "I know. I'll make it up tomorrow."

"Gee, that's great," Jessica snapped. She flounced onto her messy bed and picked at a purple satin pillowcase. "I wish I could fix my problems that fast."

Elizabeth tied off a row of stitching, snipped her thread, and set down her scissors and jeans on her bedside table. She put her hands behind her head and stretched her legs out on her pink-and-white-striped comforter. "Yeah. It's not always that easy."

"Well, it's not getting easier with Nick," Jessica hinted. She grabbed a hairbrush from the floor and yanked it through her long hair.

"You know," Elizabeth began, "when love is right, everything is right."

Jessica's mouth dropped open, and she stared up at the dingy ceiling with irritation. "Elizabeth. I'm *trying* to tell you someth—"

"When Tom and I were having problems, nothing seemed to work. Writing was harder. Classes were harder. *Life* was harder."

Jessica felt her blood boil. "What's wrong with you, Liz? Can't you see I'm upset?"

Elizabeth began giggling softly to herself. She curled on her side and gently pummeled her teddy bear's soft stomach. "I'm sorry, Jess. Really. I'm having a little trouble concentrating these days."

"Right."

"Oh! Do you know what Tom gave me today?"

"Um . . . *no*."

Her face flushing pink, Elizabeth picked something up from her bedside table. "His mother's pen. It's an heirloom. And do you know what he told me?"

"Um . . . *no*."

"He said he loved me more than ever, even though I'm not going back to WSVU. He said he understood how much I loved to write. And so he gave me the pen."

"How staggeringly romantic."

Elizabeth rolled over on her back, unfazed. "Oh, come on, Jess."

Jessica pouted and rummaged under her bed for her newest bottle of nail polish. "Oh, come on, yourself. I mean, my relationship with Nick is practically *on the rocks* and all you can talk about is Tom Terrific."

Elizabeth's blue-green eyes seemed to focus. She jolted up. "On the rocks?"

44

"Yes," Jessica said tearfully as she laid a glossy stripe of pink down the center of one nail. "All he wants to do is sit around and study."

Elizabeth shrugged. "Well, he *is* planning to go to college, Jess. That's four years. And maybe three years of law school after that. He's going to be studying a lot for a while."

"Yes, but—"

"I remember when Tom and I were first dating." Elizabeth rolled over on her stomach and gazed happily into space. "He was working like crazy on this investigative piece, and at first I . . ."

Blah, blah, blah, blah, Jessica thought miserably as Elizabeth pointed her toes into the air and danced them around. It was bad enough having a boyfriend turn into a geekster right before her eyes. But now her normally sweet and sympathetic twin was going all insensitive on her.

Tom, Tom, Tom, Tom, she complained to herself. *He's controlling Elizabeth's brain once again. Invading her every thought and feeling.* Please *let them break up soon—I need my real sister back!*

Jessica blew on her nail and tuned Elizabeth out. But she couldn't relax. Everything about the room and Elizabeth was giving her a horrendous headache. The faint smell of her sister's highlighters. The distant thump of hip-hop from the room above. The tacky dorm dressers with their chipped paint. And especially Elizabeth's happy news flashes about her perfect boyfriend.

Her head throbbing with frustration, Jessica

reached under her pillow for her Discman. She clamped on the headphones, turned on her favorite CD full blast, and closed her eyes. She would shut out everything. Everything. Except . . .

An image kept appearing and reappearing in the darkness behind her eyes. A face. A pair of eyes. A voice.

Nice night, huh?

Jessica felt a thrill in the pit of her stomach.

He's calling. He's calling. He's calling. . . .

Jessica turned off the music and stared up at the ceiling. She was seeing him all over again. Those eyes like melted chocolate. The long stretch of muscular neck. The fullness of his lips. She squirmed on her bed, imagining what it would feel like to press her own against them. To run her fingers over his smooth chest . . .

I wonder what he's doing right this very minute, Jessica mused, suddenly wishing for a way to find out. That guy was *not* sitting in a dorm room somewhere. And he was *definitely* not hunched over *How to Be a Boring College Guy,* or whatever it was that Nick was reading. . . .

Wham.

Danny slammed the door to his dorm room so hard, his wall clock crashed to the floor.

"Damn!"

He stomped over to his bed and flung his heavy backpack on the floor.

"I'm suffocating you, huh, Isabella?" Danny

muttered, balling up a fist and pounding it into the palm of his other hand. He stared angrily out the window at the lights of the campus buildings.

"Maybe I need a little air too," Danny whispered. "Maybe I need to start spending more time doing something productive." He kicked his backpack. "Like acing this microbiology class once and for all."

He stared at the smashed clock and tried to block out the image of Isabella's beautiful face. When he had first met her, he could hardly believe that a girl like her would be interested in him. *She* had actually pursued *him*. Persuaded him, even, that they were meant for each other.

After the initial shock Danny had fallen head over heels for Isabella. For the first time in his life, he had opened his heart completely to another person.

And how had Isabella repaid him?

By throwing herself on the first new guy who gets in her face, that's how.

The more Danny thought about it, the angrier he felt. It made him sick to think of the hours and hours they'd spent together. Now he knew they had been wasted. He could have been studying, or getting in shape, or windsurfing, or rewiring his car.

Danny punched the wall. His grades had suffered. And it was all because he'd let himself get swept away by a beautiful, charming woman.

Anyone could have told him that would happen.

Danny flicked on his CD player and flopped back down on his bed. It was a slow R & B tune he loved. One that reminded him of Isabella. Soft and reassuring. So beautiful . . .

He reached back to his desktop and pulled a framed picture off it. It was a picture Tom had taken of him and Isabella at the Jolly Roger Café, shortly after they'd started dating. The two of them, caught in a laughing embrace in a booth. His own love-struck face smiled back at the camera as if he'd never known a miserable day in his life. Isabella's head was nestled on his shoulder, her lovely eyes half closed and her silky black hair slipping off her white shoulder.

She was beautiful, all right.

When he looked at that photograph, it seemed as if nothing could ever come between them. Had anything ever made him as happy as Isabella had?

Danny set the frame down carefully. It was true that Isabella would always attract men. It was a fact of life, and not necessarily something he or Isabella could do anything about.

"She told me she needs a person like me to protect her," Danny whispered. "I *do* watch out for her. I *do* worry about the jerks who are only interested in what they see."

Danny sprang up from the bed and paced the floor. Giving up on Isabella wasn't the answer. She needed him to be solid and dependable, not a jealous flake. If Isabella wanted protecting, then that's what he would give her!

He thought about walking right over to Isabella's dorm and apologizing to her. He was interrupted by a knock on the door. When he opened it, Isabella herself was standing there.

"Hi," he said shortly, opening the door wider.

Isabella looked pale and impatient. "Hi, Danny."

He cleared his throat. Somehow having Isabella right there in the flesh was making his resolution more difficult. "What's up?"

"Can we talk?"

Danny motioned for her to enter. "Sure."

Isabella walked slowly over to the window, then turned around. Her eyes were red rimmed. There were two tense lines between her eyebrows he'd never seen before. "I'm not sure what happened on the quad today."

Danny pushed down the anger rising inside him. *You were crawling all over another guy, that's what happened,* he wanted to say.

"Danny?"

"I—I'm sorry," he said instead.

"Derrick and I were just joking around," Isabella said, looking at him with her clear, direct eyes. "It didn't mean anything."

Danny couldn't move. He took in every inch of her face, trying to understand it. Or maybe he was looking for cracks. He knew that because he loved her, he should believe her and trust her. And yet even though he loved Isabella, it was hard for him to trust. Maybe it wasn't something he could actually do.

"You take things the wrong way," Isabella continued. "And I don't like it. It makes me feel—I

49

don't know—sort of *guilty,* even when there's no reason for me to."

Danny could feel himself fill up with remorse and confusion. Sometimes he thought loving Isabella was the hardest thing he'd ever done. Love wasn't something he could really wrap his mind around, like a calculus test or a machine that needed fixing. It wasn't something he could finish or control. It was just always there, floating through him, unpredictable, wonderful and terrible at the same time.

Tears filled Isabella's beautiful eyes. "Do you understand?"

"Yes," Danny said quietly.

Isabella's face lightened a little, and she took a step toward him. "Let's not fight. I hate this."

Danny met her and wrapped his arms around her slender body. He kissed her, letting his lips linger on hers before finally pulling away. "I'm so sorry."

"OK," she said. Her gaze clung to his for a moment before she stepped back. She sighed and wiped a stray tear. "I've got to get back to my room and get some sleep. It's late."

"Good night, then," Danny said softly, walking her to the door as a thousand silent questions swirled in his head, unanswered.

"See you tomorrow, OK?"

"Yeah," Danny said, shutting the door. He sat down on the edge of his bed and buried his head in his hands. He *would* see her tomorrow. And the day after. He had to. From now on, he wasn't letting her out of his sight.

"You got that e-mail from that researcher in San Francisco yet?" *Gazette* editor in chief Ed Greyson asked.

"Got it five minutes ago," Elizabeth called out. "Is there any coffee left?"

"If you like the strong, syrupy kind with little flecks of burned stuff on top," advised Miko Oshima, a fellow *Gazette* writer.

"No, thanks," Elizabeth murmured. She rubbed her eyes and looked at her *Gazette* desk. A mountain of faxes, clippings, legal pads, and black-and-white photos filled her in basket. Empty cardboard coffee cups and Pringles containers surrounded her computer. Her monitor was pasted all around with yellow Post-It stickers scribbled with reminders, phone numbers, and name spellings. Even her floor was overloaded with back copies of the *Gazette*, the *L.A. Times*, and national newsmagazines.

"Check out CNN at noon, Liz," said Jane O'Donnell, the music columnist, as she breezed by. "They're doing a piece on campus gang activity."

"Thanks," Elizabeth replied. "Say, how's the new Candy Butchers album?"

Jane stopped and her face lit up. "*Amazing*. Ohhh, don't even get me started! The first song is—"

"Excuse me, Jane?" Ed interrupted. "Wasn't your copy due about, oh, a half hour ago?"

"Yeah, yeah, yeah," Jane said as she hustled back to her desk.

51

Ed walked over to Elizabeth's desk. "Where are those campus news briefs?"

Elizabeth pounded a sentence out on her keyboard and pressed the print button. She turned to Ed with a grin. "Right here. A day late—sorry."

Ed shrugged. "It's cool."

She raised her eyebrows. "My, you're in a good mood."

"I ate my Wheaties this morning."

Elizabeth pushed back her chair and smiled. Working at the *Gazette* was incredibly cool now that Scott Sinclair was gone. And it wasn't just because she finally had their cramped, shared desk all to herself.

She picked at her nail and shivered. She couldn't believe how close she had come to leaving with him for DCIR. How could she possibly have thought for one tiny moment that running off with Scott was a good idea? Sure, the school was prestigious, but so were SVU and the *Gazette*.

"Whew." She double-clicked on a word-processing icon and opened up a new document. "Tension's all gone away. *Thank* you, Scott."

"Talking to yourself again, Elizabeth?" a voice to her right asked. It belonged to the *Gazette*'s new copy editor, Nikki Tisch, who slipped a fax onto her desk.

"I heard it was allowed now," Elizabeth joked back, glancing at the fax and, a moment later, feeling her carefree smile evaporate.

The fax was from Scott Sinclair.

"Guess he hasn't forgotten you yet, huh?" Nikki said with a wink as she left.

"No," Elizabeth whispered. She scanned the message and groaned. "He's sending me a *fax*? Has he ever heard of letters? The phone? Or even an e-mail?"

Hadn't Scott realized that he was the last person in the world Elizabeth wanted to hear from?

Dear Elizabeth,

I know it's a little crazy, me sending you a fax, but I've been so busy, I haven't even had time to buy stamps. Plus, hey, a fax will get to you a lot faster. I figured you were probably pretty anxious to find out how things are at the Denver Center for Investigative Reporting. (Sounds pretty cool, huh?)

"How about *not*." Elizabeth dropped the fax down onto her lap and bit her lip. Why would she be anxious to know after all the horrible things he'd said to her?

Anyway, I don't know where to begin, except that it's awesome here. Ever hear of Tom Pickett? You know, the guy who broke that big congressional embezzlement story in D.C.? Well, he's my editor. (Bet you're jealous!) He's sort of brought me under his wing on a couple of hot stories going down here in Denver. (I'd tell you, but it's still in

53

the confidential stage. Let you know later.)

Elizabeth, I'll be honest with you. You really should be here. I mean, I hate to say this, but the little old *Gazette* isn't the right place for a talent like yours. I respect your decision, but will you think about changing your mind? I'll keep you updated. Say hello to the gang.

Love,
Scott

Elizabeth made a face and crumpled the fax under her hand. She took aim and threw it neatly into the wastebasket in the corner. Three points.

"*Love,* Scott?" Elizabeth whispered. "Hello to the *gang?*"

She sat back in her chair and stared up at the ceiling. Scott had to be one weird, mixed-up guy to send her a message like that. What did he want? Her forgiveness? Or had he just forgotten every awful thing that had happened between them?

For a long moment Elizabeth just stared into the blank, gray screen before her, feeling the last strands of regret and sadness floating away into air.

I want you out of my life, Scott, she told him in her mind. *So if you want to be nice to me, don't ever try to get in touch with me again.*

Chapter
Four

"Hurry *up*," Denise urged Isabella from the top porch step of the Theta Alpha Theta sorority house. Instead of her usual shredded jeans and T-shirt she was wearing a pink blazer over charcoal gabardine trousers. "The meeting's already started."

"Sorry," Isabella panted. She smoothed back her hair and pulled her lip gloss out of her jacket pocket. "My French lit class is miles from here. I practically jogged all the way."

"Mmm," Denise said softly as she held open the door. "Sounds convincing. But how will Her Highness, Princess Alison, take it?"

"She'll live." Isabella smoothed her lips together as she and Denise headed across the Thetas' foyer. Isabella checked her hair in the large gilt mirror hanging over a vase of fresh flowers. With a sigh she followed Denise across the shiny oak floor toward the living room, which was jammed with her Theta sisters.

"Number-one item on the agenda is that big Alpha Chi Delta cocktail party coming up this weekend," Denise whispered.

"Mmm. I'm ready for a serious party," Isabella said. "I've got a great little black dress hanging in my closet without a reason to live."

Denise nudged her in the ribs. "Mine is on its hands and knees, *begging* me to find a party."

Isabella laughed as they squeezed through the throng and searched for a pair of empty seats.

"People!" Alison Quinn stood in front of the fireplace, wearing a tailored powder blue jacket, matching pants, and an urgent expression on her face. "May we get started, please?"

A hush fell over the room as Isabella and Denise took their seats next to Jessica and Lila Fowler, whose heads were glued together in deep complaining mode. Alexandra Rollins was giggling in the back row with a new pledge while Theta president Magda Helperin watched over the whole scene, looking quietly bored.

"The first item on our agenda," Alison began primly, "is the upcoming Alpha Chi Delta event." She slipped a finger underneath her bangs and flipped them back while a murmur of approval rippled through the living room.

"As you probably know by now," Alison continued, "the Alpha Chis opened their first SVU chapter last year and are hard at work promoting their organization. So, to impress us all with their fabulous social skills, they are planning to make this event the biggest night of the year on Greek Row."

56

One of the pledges broke into uncontrollable, nervous giggles. Isabella rolled her eyes.

"The dress is semiformal," Alison said sternly, her eyes grazing the crowd, "and the Theta dress code will err on the side of formal and conservative, of course. Think elegant, simple, and classic. No dippy fluorescent colors, low-cut clothing, or dates who would be inappropriate for this kind of event."

"No bikers or ex-cons, please," Denise whispered. Isabella choked back a giggle.

"And attendance is mandatory, by the way," Alison said with a hint of a smile.

Isabella leaned toward Denise. "As *if*."

"As if anyone wouldn't *want* to go," Denise whispered back.

Alison cleared her throat and looked disapprovingly at Isabella and Denise. "Nine o'clock sharp. Saturday. Alpha Chi house." Arching her eyebrows, she made a big check mark on her notebook, then looked up again. "I have one other routine warning."

A groan rose up from the crowd.

"This is a cocktail party," Alison said. "Emphasis on the word *cocktail*. That means beer, wine, and hard liquor will be served. The key word here is *moderation*. The Thetas drink lightly. Thetas do not get drunk."

"Come on, Alison," Lila protested. "We've already been through this routine. I don't think anyone in this house has a problem with alcohol."

"Alison?" Alexandra stood up and waved her hand a little to get Alison's attention. "I have that special report you asked me to deliver, if this is a good time."

"Yes," Alison replied, gesturing for Alexandra to come to the front. "Please begin."

Alexandra strode to the front of the room, looked down at a three-by-five card in her hand, then looked up. "Alison asked me to do a little research on alcohol and drug use on campus."

"OK, Alex, get *on* with it," drawled Tina Chai, the Theta secretary.

Isabella scowled in Tina's direction. Tina and Alison were cut from the same cloth. Isabella knew Alexandra had a flirtation with alcohol and drugs back at Sweet Valley High, and she'd fallen off the wagon after her boyfriend, Mark Gathers, left SVU. Now she was completely straight and deeply committed to her work as a volunteer at the SVU hot line.

"I know you all think alcohol and drugs are not really that big a problem on the SVU campus anymore," Alexandra went on. "And certainly not a problem at Theta house. But think again."

Isabella bit her lip and sighed. Alexandra's heart was definitely in the right place, but it wasn't like her to get on a soapbox. She certainly didn't look comfortable. Why was Alison always arranging these lectures on good behavior? Between Danny and Alison, Isabella felt as if she would suffocate.

"The SVU health clinic says its referrals to alcohol rehab clinics have increased by forty-five percent in the past two years," Alexandra warned. "Serious drinking is becoming a danger on campus, and I guess I'd just like to tell everyone to be really careful. You might have heard about the girl in Oakley Hall who nearly died of alcohol poisoning last week. She's still in the hospital."

A hush fell over the room.

"Meanwhile," Alexandra went on, "I have spoken with SVU's top campus security officer, Sergeant Thomas Matlock. He explained to me that drug dealers are getting more sophisticated about penetrating markets on college campuses." She stopped, bit her bottom lip, and looked down at her notes. "College students tend to have more discretionary income and are often under the kinds of pressures that make them vulnerable to drugs."

"Like what?" Alison asked.

"Um . . ." Alexandra looked up from her notes. "Well, for example, students cramming for finals often try amphetamines and cocaine for the first time. And then there's that whole thing about trying to drink a lot of beer and party without completely crashing . . . a lot of people are taking uppers for that."

"Nasty," Lila murmured.

"Yuck," Denise agreed.

"So . . ." Alexandra looked back down at her card. "Yeah. Um. So to make a long story short, a lot of dealers in the southern California area are hitting the campuses harder—with everything—marijuana, cocaine . . . even heroin."

"What Alexandra is trying to say," Alison broke in, clasping her hands, "is just watch yourselves, ladies. Thetas do *not* do drugs. They don't experiment with drugs. They don't try drugs once. They don't even *look* at drugs or the people who use them. OK?"

"Alison?" Debbie Sharp, a new pledge, waved her hand in the air. "Why are we even *talking* about this? I mean, drugs are so totally destructive and stupid and déclassé. *Thetas* are not into this kind of thing, right?"

"Hey, our own Jessica Wakefield was mixed up in a cocaine bust not too long ago, it seems to me . . . ," Tina whispered loudly.

Isabella and Denise shared a disgusted look.

"Hey!" Jessica cried. "Everyone knows I was—"

"Yes, we *all* know you were innocent, Jessica," Alison said with a smug smile. "So let's not have any reminders, OK? Thank you for that report, Alexandra. You may sit down."

"But wait a minute, Alison," Alexandra protested. "I don't think we should just write off the subject of drugs because we think we're too good for them."

"We *are* too good for them. And it's not our *issue*," Alison snapped. "Debbie is right. May we move on now?"

"It's an issue if we can't even talk about it," Alexandra came back, still standing, a defiant pink flush creeping up her cheeks.

Isabella sat back in her chair and closed her eyes. *I can't take it!* she thought in frustration. Why did everyone—Danny Wyatt, especially—have to be so serious all the time? She was sick of everyone trying to protect and shelter her from all the wickedness of the world.

She knew one thing for sure—she didn't want to take Danny to the cocktail party, even though she knew she'd have to. He'd do everything in his power to make sure she was the only one not having fun. And a little wicked fun was *exactly* what she needed.

"Done!" Elizabeth sat on the edge of Ed Greyson's desk. "It's in the Thursday news file under campus news briefs."

"Thanks," he said, gulping his coffee as he scrolled up his directory. "You're a lifesaver."

"Gotta get to my one o'clock," Elizabeth said hurriedly, glancing at her watch.

"Do you still have that file on Coach Warner?" Ed asked.

"Oh yeah." Elizabeth hefted her leather backpack onto her shoulder. "Let me grab it off my desk."

Elizabeth hurried back and quickly sifted through a stack of folders until she spotted the file. But just as she was about to rush off, her phone rang. Reluctantly she picked it up.

"Elizabeth?"

She gasped.

"Elizabeth! I know it's you. Did you get my fax? How much do you miss me? Elizabeth?"

The sound of Scott Sinclair's voice sent a strange chill through her body. Her elbow felt frozen in place. Her lips were paralyzed in midair.

"Elizabeth? Hello?"

What was she supposed to do? Act like she was happy to hear from him?

Never.

"E-*liz*-a-beth. Where *are* you?"

She thought she would be sick. What did Scott want from her? Before she left the plane, he practically told her she was worthless without him.

Well, Scott, I'm not with you, Elizabeth thought. *And I'm not worthless. So can we just end this, please?*

For a moment her mind raced with indecision. And then, as the memory of his angry, bitter face came into focus, she realized there was really no decision to make at all.

She hung up the phone without saying a word.

"What a waste of time," Jessica muttered as she hurried down Greek Row. Alison's meeting had turned into a pointless debate on how to penalize Theta sisters who experimented with drugs, even if it only happened once.

Alison was all for immediate and permanent expulsion from the sorority. Isabella and Alexandra insisted that the Theta sorority was a sisterhood that should support and counsel its fallen members.

"Give me a break," Jessica muttered, rushing past the other stately Greek houses, each one bordered by neat hedges and rows of shiny parked cars—no old beaters in sight.

Jessica loved being a part of the Greek system. She loved the parties. She loved the Thetas, if only because Theta house was the top house and her mother was totally happy she'd followed in her hallowed Theta footsteps. Being a Theta made her feel good.

But enough about the drugs already, Jessica thought with irritation. OK. Drugs were bad. She'd been around enough to know. So why did everyone insist on bringing up how she accidentally stumbled into one of Nick's stings? It wasn't as if she was taking drugs, and she *definitely* wasn't selling them— that's what she had been falsely accused of. But on the SVU campus the word *cocaine* had somehow become indelibly linked to the name Jessica Wakefield.

"Everyone, please give it a rest," she muttered as she stomped toward the dining hall, where she was planning to meet Elizabeth for an early dinner. Elizabeth would understand her frustration—if she finally stopped daydreaming about Mr. Wonderful for ten minutes.

She cut onto the pathway past the pond. She breathed in the smell of freshly mowed grass and ordered herself to remove all negative thoughts from her head.

Jessica sighed heavily. It was impossible. After all, her world was totally cracking up. Nick was a nerd. The Thetas were putting her to sleep. And everything—*everything*—in her life had been the *same, same, same* for *weeks*.

Even the glamorous Alpha Chi Delta cocktail party loomed as a possible disaster on the horizon.

After all, she'd be taking Nick—a risky move. She could just picture Nick butting into happy conversations with commentary on philosophy and prelaw requirements.

As she emerged from the quad and rounded the corner toward the dining hall, even the steady click of her footsteps bored her. Wondering about what would be served for dinner bored her. The thought of hearing another cheerful story about Tom bored her.

Up ahead, the sound of a lone harmonica broke through Jessica's thoughts. She stopped and listened. It was a slow, sexy song that made Jessica think of long, lonely train whistles and lovers' farewells. A delicious shiver went up her back.

The music broke, and Jessica took a few steps forward until she had made it around the building's corner and could see the concrete bench and landscaping that edged the patio outside the dining hall.

She slowed when she saw a figure alone on the bench. The music started up once again.

Jessica froze. Though the light was dim, she could clearly make out the face—a face she realized she knew already. A face she'd been dreaming about all night. The guy she'd met in front of the library!

When the harmonica's song stopped again, Jessica felt her heart speed up. She took another step forward into the light that spilled out of the windows.

"Hey, there," the guy called out.

Jessica straightened and walked toward him, feeling her old confidence take over. "Do I know you?" she demanded.

He winked and stuck his harmonica into his back pocket. "Not yet."

Jessica opened her mouth to speak, but no sound came out.

"Cat got your tongue?" The guy stood up and walked toward her. He was tall, about six feet. His longish brown hair was pulled back in a loose ponytail. Jessica was absolutely sure she had never seen brown eyes that were deeper than his—set like two soft pools over smooth, olive cheekbones. Like yesterday, he was wearing a dark T-shirt and jeans.

"And who are you?" Jessica asked, lifting one eyebrow.

The guy shook his head slowly as his eyes roamed up and down her body. "You go first."

Jessica shivered. "No. You first."

He smiled as if he were slightly shy, though Jessica was definitely sure he wasn't. "I always let the ladies go first."

Jessica stepped closer. "Well, that's too bad, because I *always* get my way."

For a long second the guy let his eyes hang on to her gaze. "Clay," he finally said.

Jessica tipped her head to one side and smiled. "Clay what?"

"Clay DiPalma."

"Hi, Clay," Jessica said.

Clay drew one hand out of his pocket and took Jessica's. He lifted it to his lips and gently kissed it.

Jessica's pulse pounded in her ears. She prayed Clay couldn't hear it. Slowly she pulled her hand away and looked into his eyes. "Anything else?" she asked coolly. Far more coolly than she felt.

He gestured toward the bench. "Talk to me," he said softly.

"OK." Jessica felt his hand press delicately against the small of her tingling back. She let him lead her to the bench, where she sat down and slowly crossed her legs. She smiled and looked him over, her heart hammering in her chest like it hadn't in ages. The thought made her start. How long had it been? Ever since she'd first met Nick?

It was true, Jessica realized. Since Nick had come into her life, no one else had made her blood boil like the stranger sitting next to her. What did it mean? Was it what she really wanted?

"Want to know something?" Clay asked, moving closer to her.

"What?" Jessica murmured, shivering as if he'd just blown into her ear. There was something— well, a little *twisted* about this guy. What it was, she wasn't exactly sure. But she definitely didn't want to tear herself away anytime soon.

"You haven't told me your name."

Jessica smiled mysteriously. "What do you *think* my name is?"

"Jessica."

Jessica's eyes opened wide. "How did you know?"

"I asked." Clay slipped his arm along the back of the bench until his hand brushed the nape of Jessica's neck.

Jessica frowned. She didn't like the idea of a mysterious stranger asking around about her. "Why didn't you just ask me?"

Clay held up his hands. "Sorry. Guess I just figured you'd blow me off."

Jessica gave him a hard stare. "Where'd you get that idea?" she asked.

He shrugged. "So . . . what are you doing for dinner, Jessica?"

"Nothing," she lied quickly, to her surprise.

"Come on, then," Clay urged her, sneaking his fingers into Jessica's palm. "Let's get out of here."

"Whoa." Jessica pushed down his hand. "Not so fast."

"Why not?"

Jessica flipped back a wedge of her hair and looked him in the eye. "I don't go wandering off with guys I don't know anything about."

"Yes, you do." Clay's direct expression threw Jessica off for a moment. But then he smiled, revealing deep dimples in his cheeks and a row of very white teeth. "You don't seem like the kind of girl who follows all the rules."

Jessica smiled and let her eyes roam languidly over his body. This guy was getting *very* interesting. She connected with his gaze again. "Well, you may be right about that."

"I know I am," Clay replied, touching her chin lightly with his thumb.

Jessica suddenly felt light-headed, and she laughed. This Clay DiPalma was *just* the kind of guy who could turn a boring Greek cocktail party into an unforgettable night.

"Hey, how's it going?" Nick asked as he rapped on Chief Wallace's open office door.

"It's The Fox!" Chief Wallace boomed. He waved him off as his phone rang.

"Nick's here!" the chief's secretary exclaimed.

Nick waved as he strolled farther down the hall to his old office, where his former partner, Dub Harrison, was crouched next to a file cabinet, digging through a set of papers. He took a deep breath. The station smelled like stale coffee and cigarette butts. "Hey, Dub."

Dub Harrison grinned as he stood up. He was a stocky guy who wore short-sleeved dress shirts that strained along the button line. His beefy face was red, and he was breathing hard through the thick cigar he held between his teeth. "How's Mr. College Boy?"

"Not there yet, Dub." Nick leaned against the doorjamb. "But I'm working on it. I spent some time at the library last night—really ticked Jessica off."

Dub laughed. "The lovely Miss Wakefield won't put up with that dull business for long, Fox."

Nick cleared his throat. Dub had a habit of stating the obvious stuff he didn't want to face.

His old partner puffed on his cigar. "Stuck my foot in my mouth again, huh?"

Nick slapped down his hand, sat down in Dub's chair, and swiveled around. "No way."

Dub shut the filing cabinet. "Thinking about coming back yet?"

Nick shook his head. "Just strolled downtown for a burger and decided to check up on my old colleagues. Perfectly innocent."

"Well, you were cut out for bigger things." Dub clapped his hand on Nick's shoulder. "Wish you were still here. Could use you."

"What's going on?"

Dub shrugged. "I don't know. I just got a tip on a new crop of low-grade dealers coming into town. They're pumping some cheap stuff onto those campus kids. I don't like it."

"I'll keep an eye out," Nick promised him, glancing around. "Hey, this place is giving me the creeps," he joked. "I'm out of here."

"Sure thing, Fox," Dub said with a salute.

Nick slung his coat over his shoulder and sauntered out of the office past the pay phones, soda machines, and a huddle of young kids in knit caps being hustled in for bookings. Outside, the air was fresh, and Nick had a sudden desire to find Jessica—even if he could see her only for a moment. He didn't like the way he left things with her after the library last night. She seemed so distant. Maybe Dub was right. . . .

He checked his watch again. He knew that Jessica was usually having dinner about now. If he hurried, he might catch her.

A few moments later Nick was in his Camaro, heading toward the shady green of the SVU campus.

He tapped the steering wheel impatiently, his thoughts filled with the image of Jessica's irritated face yesterday morning after her philosophy class.

Nick raked his dark hair back with his hand. It wasn't the first time Nick suspected something was going on with Jessica. After all, he was six years older than she was. She was just an innocent college freshman. Well, *sort of* innocent. Anyway, she was a beautiful girl, surrounded by good-looking guys every day. And all of them were ready to pounce if she gave them the slightest invitation. That much he was sure of.

The campus visitors' parking lot was only a few hundred yards from the dining hall. Nick's stomach gave a sudden growl, and his mood lifted. Cafeteria food wasn't so bad—and at those prices he could afford it. He whistled as he got out of the car, locked the door, and sauntered down the walkway, jingling the change in his pocket.

The light in the sky had begun to fall, and the walkway lamps winked on. Up ahead, he could see the yellow light pouring from the dining hall's picture windows. Knots of students were moving toward the entrance, and a few stragglers waited on the broad patio. Nick squinted. At its edge, on a low bench, he could barely make out the dim figure of a girl sitting next to a lanky, long-haired guy.

Slowly and without realizing it, he stopped. Something was wrong, and he felt his instincts kicking in—taking in the girl's description, checking the time, the place, the exact situation. . . .

Jessica?

He stared in disbelief. The guy she was sitting next to was obviously coming on to her, and Jessica was eating it up. He *knew* she was. She always flipped her hair back like that when she was flirting. That's what she used to do with *him!* He could see the distinct arch of her back and then . . . *then* the guy leaning forward and touching her face.

And Jessica wasn't doing a damn thing about it.

Suddenly Nick's feet were moving down the walkway. He could feel his heart race and his face heat up with a strange kind of anger he hadn't felt in a long time.

"Jessica!" he shouted, taking the steps to the patio two at a time. "What's going on?"

He watched as Jessica's laughing face fell. She turned and looked over her shoulder as if she were actually *irritated* by the interruption. "Nick?"

"Yeah, Nick," he said, trying to hold back his rage. He rushed forward as the guy pulled away from Jessica, glared, and stood up to face him.

"Who is this nutcase, Jessica?" the guy demanded.

"Hey." Nick stepped up to the guy, practically nose to nose. "Watch it, buddy."

The guy stepped back in mock horror. "Whoa. Jessica. Protect me."

"Stop it, Clay. This is my boyfriend, Nick Fox," Jessica said with an irritated glance at Nick.

"Oooh," Clay drawled. "So Jessica's got a big bad sugar daddy, huh?"

Nick suddenly saw red flash in front of his eyes, and his right arm tensed. The guy was trouble. He could feel it in his gut. He balled up his fist and smashed the guy in the jaw, knocking him to the ground.

"Nick!" Jessica screamed. She looked down in horror at the guy's body. For a split second Nick thought he saw something open up in Jessica's face. At first he thought it was surprise. Then he saw that it was admiration, though it quickly turned into anger.

"What the hell is this about, Jessica?"

"Nothing happened!" she shouted, attracting the attention of several students who'd clustered nearby. "We were just talking. I just met him!"

Slowly the guy pulled himself up from the ground and rubbed his jaw angrily.

"Let's get out of here. *Now,*" Nick shouted. He grabbed Jessica's arm.

"Let go of me!" she cried.

"I'll let go of you as soon as I get that guy out of my sight."

Nick watched as the guy staggered away into the darkness, his eyes flashing with anger. Holding his jaw with one hand, he pointed at Nick with the other. "You just asked for it, buddy," he muttered hoarsely.

Chapter Five

"Nick! Stop!"

"We need to talk, Jessica." Nick tightened his grip around her shoulders and half dragged her toward the parking lot.

Jessica had to run to keep up with Nick's long strides. "Slow down! You're way over the line, Nick. Stop it."

Nick suddenly froze, and he pressed his fingers against his forehead. His breathing was hard and shallow. "OK, Jess. OK."

Jessica had never seen Nick like this. His face was flushed with anguish, and for a split second she thought she actually saw tears in his green eyes. Her spine tingled with excitement. "You totally punched that guy out," she said, licking her lips and practically panting at the memory.

Nick shook his head. "I know. I know. I shouldn't have done that. I—just couldn't help myself."

Jessica's heart was pounding, and she felt a delicious warmth wash over her. She took a step toward Nick and ran a finger down the front of his leather jacket. "We were just *talking*, you know."

Nick grabbed her shoulders and looked into her face, his eyes wet with emotion. "I know what you were doing, and I can't stand it."

Jessica was about to protest when Nick suddenly kissed her hard on the mouth. His brawny arms wrapped around her body tightly. She was dizzy with ecstasy. Nick was himself again: passionate, forceful—a real man! Was a little jealousy all it took to bring back his manly, bad-boy passion? Why hadn't she thought of it before?

Jessica pulled away from his kiss. "Actually," she whispered breathlessly, "I was glad you showed up."

Nick pulled her close again, his eyes burning. "Good." He closed his eyes, still breathing hard. "Don't do that to me again."

Jessica put a finger to his lips. Her knees practically buckled with joy. "I won't."

"Jess?"

"Shhh." Jessica wrapped her arms around his neck and kissed him again. She melted against his strong chest and into his powerful arms. Nick Fox wasn't a romantic fantasy, Jessica suddenly realized. He was a real person with real passion and bravery. She didn't have to imagine that he was someone else because he was everything she wanted—even if he had weird ideas about his future. She loved him with all her heart. How could she have forgotten, even for a moment?

"You were good out there, you know," Jessica said as she came up for air. "You were really . . . hot."

Nick pulled away for a moment and looked at her in confusion. "Hot?"

With a long sigh Jessica took Nick's hand and led him down the walkway toward his car. "You know what I mean. You're the kind of guy other guys have to watch out for. I mean, you can be dangerous when you want to."

Nick shrugged. "I suppose."

Jessica swung his hand back and forth "I've been missing that, you know."

"Missing what?"

"My wild guy."

Nick's stern expression began to break up. "The big, bad cop you love so much?"

"Yeah," Jessica said. "I thought I'd lost him."

Nick nodded and looked up at the sky. "You thought I'd turned into that ink-stained prelaw student with the bag of books and those annoying philosophical questions."

Jessica stopped walking. "Well . . . *yeah.*"

Nick turned to her and slipped his fingers through her hair. His green eyes glittering, he tipped her head back for another long, lingering kiss. "I'm still me. OK? Still the same old Nick. That's not going to change."

"I hope not."

"Sorry I don't always let my wild side show, Jess," Nick said, a smile escaping out of the corner of his mouth before he dipped down for a final, toe-tingling kiss.

"Oh, Nick," Jessica breathed.

"Mmmm."

"There's a big party this Saturday night at the Alpha Chi Delta house. A cocktail party. Very fancy. You going to come with me or not?"

"Oh yeah," Nick said softly. He ran his knuckle down the side of her face. "I'll be there, all right."

"For those of you over on the east side of the roof," announced Professor Wiley, the SVU astronomy club's adviser, "you have an excellent opportunity to observe the planet Mars."

"I found it!" Elizabeth cried, waving Tom over. She steadied the telescope with her slender hands. Lined up next to her were several other students, all of them peering into telescopes set up on the roof of Larkin Hall, the astrophysics building.

"Let's see." Tom slipped his arm around her waist.

Elizabeth didn't move. "No, wait. Hey! I can see several Martian canals. And look at all of those craters."

Tom grinned. Curiosity was one of Elizabeth's top-ten strong points. And now it looked as if astronomy were about to be added to her long list of interests. Sometimes Tom felt as if he could never keep up with Elizabeth. But he knew he wouldn't have her any other way.

Elizabeth was waving one hand in the air, her eye still glued to the telescope. "You can actually see a polar ice cap," she cried.

"Excellent," Professor Wiley said, hurrying over with her clipboard and flashlight in hand. "The ice is actually frozen carbon dioxide."

"Dry ice," Elizabeth breathed, pulling away and motioning to Tom. "Check it out."

Actually, all Tom wanted to check out was Elizabeth herself. She looked so beautiful and serene as she stood there in the starlight, her blond ponytail blowing in the light breeze, her blue-green eyes luminous even in the dim light. He kissed her nose and looked at the view of Mars, then offered the telescope back to her.

"What's the matter?" Elizabeth spoke, moving the lens up to a higher spot in the Thursday night sky. "You hungry already?"

"Mind reader."

"OK," Elizabeth finally said, giving the telescope to the next person in the line. She rubbed her eyes. "It's too beautiful a night here on Earth to be looking at something a million miles away."

Tom slipped his hand into hers and led her to a secluded spot on the roof, where a small bench had been placed near the roof exit. "Please sit down, miss. Your dinner will be ready in one moment."

"Thank you," Elizabeth answered.

Tom unzipped his pack and pulled out a thick plastic-wrapped sandwich. He looked at it for a moment before handing it to her with a flourish.

"Seven grain, apple, and Brie with mustard . . . hold the pickles."

She laughed. "Perfect."

Tom pulled out a second sandwich and sat down. "Rye, roast beef, horseradish, mayo, and lettuce."

"What's for dessert?"

"This." Tom kissed her lightly on the lips.

"Mmm."

Tom leaned against Elizabeth and stretched his legs. The SVU campus at night looked like a small city spread out before them, with thousands of yellow lights twinkling from the dorms and academic buildings. In the quad, far below, he could hear the laughter of students leaving the library. And in the far distance he could hear the roar of cars on the freeway winding into the city.

He turned and faced Elizabeth, who was dabbing the corner of her mouth with a napkin. It was true that the two of them had wasted too much precious time bickering, miscommunicating, and hurting each other. But now he knew it was all in the past. He loved Elizabeth with every fiber of his soul, and he knew that she loved him back.

"What?" Elizabeth whispered, touching his leg.

Tom chewed and swallowed. His chest seemed to swell with feelings he couldn't quite describe. "I just love you. That's all."

Elizabeth leaned into him. "I love you too, Tom. Nothing can ever pull us apart again."

Tom nodded, but another thought—distant and

painful—suddenly emerged. He shut his eyes as if he could block it out.

"Something wrong?" Elizabeth said gently.

He turned and gazed at her face. So lovely and understanding. "No."

"Mmm."

Tom bit his lower lip. His head told him he had to be honest—completely honest—if his relationship with Elizabeth was going to be a long and happy one. Yet his heart told him something different. It reminded him that the truth had the awful power to hurt the person he loved. And the thought of hurting Elizabeth was unbearable. Completely unbearable.

"So, what is it?"

Tom took a big bite out of his sandwich and chewed.

"Whew," Elizabeth whistled. "Is this conversation over?"

"It's nothing, really," Tom lied, his eyes not quite meeting hers.

"OK."

Tom gave Elizabeth a quick, nervous glance. Her face seemed cheerful enough. Maybe she *hadn't* picked up on his weird mood, though he was beginning to wish she had. He needed some kind of an opening.

Tom finished his sandwich and rolled the plastic wrap between his hands until it was a tight ball. He kept thinking about honesty. Sure, the truth was the thing that could free *him* from his conscience.

But what about Elizabeth? It wouldn't free her. It would only push her away.

Of course, people were always doing things they regretted, Tom reminded himself. And usually they were forgiven. So what was he afraid of anyway?

"Come on," Elizabeth said, slipping her arm around his waist. "Spill."

"It—it's just that it feels so good to be together with you again," Tom whispered into her ear.

"I know," she whispered back.

He kissed her then. He was glad he did. Elizabeth always made him feel as if he could climb mountains. Yet he knew the kiss would only last for moments. When he pulled away, a part of him would be alone again. Alone with something he couldn't bear to reveal. Alone.

"Hand me my calculator?" Danny asked. He shifted on the floor of his dorm room and leaned his back against his bed.

Isabella lay stretched out on Danny's bed, reading her sociology textbook and sipping a latte. Her pale skin glowed against the white sleeves of her shirt, and her black hair spilled luxuriously over her shoulders.

"Catch," she said, reaching for the calculator and tossing it into Danny's open palm.

Danny's eyes met Isabella's and stayed there. He loved to be with her like this, alone in the cool and the quiet of his room. Things between them were always so easy and uncomplicated when there was no one else around to distract them. When there were no decisions to be made. No arrangements. No compromises.

He loved to imagine, in fact, that he and Isabella lived on a remote Pacific island, surrounded only by the warm sun and air. He fantasized about building a small grass house and spending long evenings by the fire with no one to interrupt their love.

"Let's go get something to eat," Isabella suggested. She slipped off the bed and crawled over to him. "I'm starved."

Danny looked at his watch. "We've only been studying for an hour. And you have an exam tomorrow."

Isabella groaned and snuggled up next to him. "I've never been more prepared for a soc test before in my life." She got up and ran her finger impatiently down a stack of Danny's CDs.

"Come on, Izzy," Danny said, forcing a smile. "Not now. OK?"

Isabella rolled her eyes and sank back down next to him. Her hair smelled faintly of flowers. "I won't blast music in your ears if you promise me one thing."

Danny looked down at her and touched the tip of her nose. "And what is that, my child?"

Isabella leaned her head on his shoulder. "I want you to promise you will go with me to the Alpha Chi Delta cocktail party Saturday night."

Danny stiffened. "Come on, Izzy. You know I don't like gigs like that." He looked up and moaned. "All the people. The small talk. Ugh. Pointless."

Isabella ran her hand down the front of his shirt. "What about that beautiful suit you have hanging in your closet? You've never worn it, have you?"

"Forget it," Danny replied, crossing his arms tightly across his muscular chest.

Isabella frowned and pulled away. She hugged her knees and sank down her forehead.

"I warned you when we first started going out," Danny tried to explain, "I'm just not that kind of guy. I don't do the social scene. I have trouble talking to a hundred people at once."

"You talk to *one person at a time*," Isabella reminded him, her voice tensing.

Danny just shook his head. "I'm not into it."

"Would you do it for me, then?" Isabella asked him softly. "It would mean a lot to me. All my Theta sisters are going. It's a really big night for us."

Danny felt his anger rising. "I didn't join the Thetas. *You* did."

Isabella's jaw dropped. "But I can't go without a date!"

"Then don't go!"

Isabella stood up and placed her hands on her hips, her gray eyes flashing. "Danny Wyatt, you're being selfish and immature. This is important to me, OK? I have an obligation to my sorority to attend this event. I have a life too, you know. I'm not just Isabella. I'm a big complicated package that comes with a lot of other things. . . ."

Danny nodded. "Don't remind me."

"I have friends and academic work and interests

and organizations I've made commitments to," Isabella went on sharply. She turned and gathered up her papers and books, which she began stuffing into her leather book bag. "And I can't just drop everything because you want to do what *you* want all the time. Sometimes I need you to do things for me too."

"I do!"

Isabella zipped up her bag and glared at him. "You're totally insecure is what you are. That's why you want me all for yourself. You can't stand to see me talking to other guys or—or spend time doing something you can't understand."

"You're wrong."

Isabella pointed at him. "You'd just love to keep me in your little cage, wouldn't you?"

Danny stood up and faced her down. "Stop it."

"*You* stop it."

Danny chewed the inside of his cheek and looked away, his foot tapping nervously on the floor. "Look. Maybe you're right about one thing anyway."

Isabella opened her mouth and took two steps backward, feigning surprise.

Danny cleared his throat uncomfortably. "You're right about having an obligation to your sorority."

Isabella's expression softened, but she said nothing.

He shrugged. "If you have to go, you have to go."

"With a date," she reminded him.

"What time?"

"Pick me up at nine o'clock sharp tomorrow night. Suit and tie." Isabella gave him a wary look as

83

she slipped the strap of her bag over her shoulder. She headed for the door. "Don't study too hard."

"I won't," Danny said lightly. He shook his head after the door closed. "And I'll definitely hang with you at the Theta party, Isabella. I wouldn't want anyone else to."

Chapter Six

"Come on, check out this part of the tape," Tom told Elizabeth. He gestured toward an empty chair in WSVU's dark editing room.

Elizabeth set down her backpack and grinned. Her one o'clock literature class had just ended, and the WSVU studio was the perfect place to hang before heading to her Friday afternoon history seminar on the other side of campus.

"What's the big deal?" Elizabeth asked. She grabbed the chair and wheeled it over to the narrow desk in front of the bank of editing machines.

Tom dimmed the light, punched the rewind button, then pushed play. Elizabeth watched as the tape revealed a picture of a campus security guard talking with a young guy wearing jeans and a hooded sweatshirt. "Where's this?" Elizabeth asked.

"Basement of the campus administration building," Tom murmured. "Right next to the registrar's data center." He gave Elizabeth a meaningful look. "You know, where student files, including grades, are stored."

"Wow," Elizabeth breathed. "Look at the time on this tape—three o'clock in the morning. How did you get this?"

Tom pushed the fast-forward button and grinned. "There's a vent in the men's room that faces the entrance to the data center, which I found *very* convenient."

"So you hooked up the minicam and set it on time lapse for the night," Elizabeth said excitedly.

Tom nodded. "Just to see what I could see. I'd heard my share of stories. . . ."

"Bingo," Elizabeth said in a hushed voice. "Look at that. That guy with the hood walks right in."

"And comes out an hour later." Tom leaned back in his chair and passed Elizabeth a bag of chips. "I figure he pays off the security guard with a relatively modest fee, then charges big bucks for a few very desperate grade changes. It's going to be a great story."

Elizabeth nodded. "I love that little camera."

Tom nudged her. "Can't really use it down at the *Gazette*, can you?"

Elizabeth reached over and switched on the light. The cramped editing room was littered with marked-up videotapes, crumpled candy bar wrappers, and clipboards. "I sure could."

"Well, you can't have it."

Elizabeth laughed. "I really do miss being here, you know. There's nothing like using a good image to tell a story."

"Yeah." Tom ejected the tape and bounced it nervously between his hands.

"Hi, Liz!" said Charles Cash, one of WSVU's senior researchers, as he ducked his head into the editing room. "Are you back?"

Elizabeth leaned back in her chair. "Wouldn't you like to know?" she teased.

"Elizabeth's back!" cheered Miki Dubonney, a frizzy-haired editor, as she joined Charles. "That totally rocks."

"Just visiting, Miki." Elizabeth stood up and stuck her hands in her pockets. She wandered out into the station's soundproof booth. "Hey, check this out! You guys finally got that new dubbing mike."

"Yeah!" Miki said. "And a new computer too." She nodded toward the station's infamous beat-up couch, where Tom and Elizabeth had spent plenty of intimate "study breaks" together. "We still haven't replaced this, though."

Elizabeth ran her hand over the shiny new keyboard. "You guys are really coming up in the world. Maybe I *will* have to come back . . . just to keep your heads from swelling." She turned to share a smile with Tom. He was leaning intently over an open file, apparently searching for something.

"Any caffeine-laced liquids in that broken-down old fridge?" Elizabeth asked. She slipped her arms around Tom's chest from behind. "I could use one right now."

"Oh yeah." Tom shut the file drawer and turned

to face her. "That much hasn't changed since you left us."

"Mmm," Elizabeth murmured. "I feel like I've only been gone for a few days."

"It seems like a lot longer," Tom said quietly.

"It feels normal to be here," Elizabeth said, sighing. She reached up and brushed a stray strand of brown hair out of Tom's eyes. "Maybe you're right. Maybe I should just pack my little laptop, say good-bye to the *Gazette,* and come back here."

"Uh-huh," Tom said. He looked down at his file and walked away.

For a moment Elizabeth just stood in the middle of the office, wondering if she'd said something wrong. But how could that be? Tom had been begging her to come back to the station.

She followed Tom into the editing room. "What I mean is . . . maybe I should think about it."

"Yeah," Tom said lightly. He sat down and flipped through the papers in the manila file. "Think about it."

"I will," Elizabeth said softly, staring at him as he stuffed another tape into the machine. From where she was standing, she could see his jaw clench just under his ear. "Guess I better get to my three o'clock. Starts in fifteen minutes. I've got a major hike to the west side of campus."

"Yeah," Tom said, turning and giving her a stiff smile. "OK."

"See you tonight," she whispered.

"OK."

Elizabeth picked up her backpack and walked slowly out of the station. She loved Tom. And she knew he loved her too. Working together again at WSVU would be a chance for them to be even closer. It would be a good thing, she realized.

So why was he suddenly acting like he didn't want her to come back?

As soon as Elizabeth was gone, Tom began working furiously on the computer grade scam story. He placed several calls to the registrar's office. One to university security. Then another to the dean of students.

So far, no one was willing to talk.

Tom leaned back in his chair and rubbed his sore neck muscles. He'd been looking forward to getting Elizabeth back in for a visit. But it had seemed so—strange.

"Any luck with those interviews?" Miki asked. She was dumping the wastebaskets into a plastic trash bag. "You've been at it for at least two hours."

"Nope," Tom said. He walked out of the room and pulled his crumpled denim jacket off the old couch. "No one in the registrar's office will talk. I guess they think I'm trying to crack their computer secrets."

"Drag."

"Yeah. Well, someone's going to have to say something sooner or later," Tom said quietly. "Especially after they see the tape I made of their security breach."

"Got your beeper?" Miki reminded him.

Tom patted his back pocket. "Yeah. I'll know it if I get any voice mail."

"See you," Miki said.

"Later," Tom muttered. He slipped out the door and headed back to his dorm. Outside, he rubbed his eyes and breathed in a lungful of fresh air. At five o'clock the campus was in that quiet, in-between-classes-and-dinner mode that he loved. A lone skater flew by, followed by a woman on a bicycle. Two women practiced tai chi near the fountain. A collarless golden retriever sniffed a bench leg, then pranced happily toward the library entrance.

Still, Tom couldn't really enjoy any of the ambiance. Too much was weighing on his mind. He let out a strange, crazy laugh he didn't even recognize as his own.

The whole thing was too weird, he decided. For months, even when he was dating beautiful Dana Upshaw, he'd longed for Elizabeth. Dreamed about her. Hoped for her. Loved her.

Tom pushed the heel of his hand hard into his forehead. "Now she's finally back," he whispered to himself. "And you don't know what you're doing anymore."

He shook his head. *What* can *I do?* he asked himself.

Tom took another deep breath as he drew near his dorm. He hurried up the steps, forcing himself to think only good thoughts. Like Elizabeth's beautiful smile. The play of her wonderful mind.

That little thing she did with her ankle when she was reading something really good.

"Hey, Watts."

He turned. His roommate, Danny Wyatt, had just finished locking up his bike at the rack in front of Reid Hall. He hurried toward Tom and gave him a light slap on the back when he caught up. "Check your mail yet?" Danny asked as they walked into the lobby past the mailboxes.

"Oh yeah," Tom said absently, digging into his pocket for his mailbox key. "Almost forgot."

Danny chuckled as he opened his own mailbox. "Whew, man. You've been down at that station too long. Admit it."

"You're right," Tom mumbled as he drew out several envelopes. "My eyes feel like two rocks. My neck feels like a rusty old hinge."

"Maybe you're in the wrong line of business," Danny joked.

"Yeah, right," Tom said. "Barking up the wrong tree."

"How's it going with Liz?"

"Great," Tom said as he flipped through the envelopes. "We're catching dinner tonight."

"Oh, man," Danny muttered. He studied a piece of mail as they headed up a flight of stairs together. "That dinner with Isabella last week just about wiped out my bank account."

"She's worth it," Tom said slowly. He opened a hand-addressed envelope, scanned the short message inside, and cursed angrily.

"What?"

"My dad," Tom said, still staring at the note as Danny unlocked their room and pushed open the door. "George. He's—he's moved."

"Where?"

"Uh." Tom looked at the note again. "San Francisco."

"Old Mr. Conroy and his disappearing act again, huh?"

Tom sat down on his bed. George Conroy was his father, but Tom hadn't known him until recently. At first he'd been thrilled to be reunited with George, a wealthy attorney with two great kids. But things soured after he'd made a pass at Elizabeth, then tried to deny it. The whole mess had caused too much pain for Tom ever to forgive him. Sighing, he read through the letter again.

Dear Tom,

Just a brief note to let you know that the kids and I are leaving tomorrow for San Francisco. I've had an offer to head the litigation department of a firm there, and I can't turn it down.

Mary and Jake send their very best and hope you'll drop them a note from time to time. Our address there for the time being will be 2045 Gough St.

Hope all goes well with your classes and your work at WSVU this year. How is our beautiful Elizabeth?

Tom's jaw dropped. He looked up from the letter in disgust. George had the gall to bring up Elizabeth? *Our beautiful Elizabeth?* Was he *nuts?*

He took a deep breath before rereading the rest.

> Please give her my very, very warmest wishes. And, if you wouldn't mind, tell her to visit if she is ever in San Francisco—or call me if she needs anything at all.
>
> Fondly,
> Dad

Tom crumpled up the note and looked up at Danny. "I'm glad he's gone."

Danny nodded. "Yeah. The guy was trouble."

"I'll miss those kids, though," Tom said, staring at his desk, which was cluttered with stacks of textbooks and half-finished papers. His computer screen saver danced in the dim light. "I was crazy about them, Danny."

"Yeah."

Tom dropped his head into his hands. "They're probably more confused than ever. You know, I really would have liked to have said good-bye to them."

"He was bad news, man," Danny said quietly, batting a basketball between his hands.

Tom stood up and stripped off his sweatshirt. "Kind of wish things had worked out with the old guy."

"I figured that."

93

"Yeah." Tom grabbed a towel and headed for the showers down the hall. But the sight of the bare, wet tiles just made him feel worse. He turned on the water, as hot as he could stand it, and tried to calm the confusion in his head. All he knew was that he needed badly to talk to Elizabeth.

And that he dreaded it more than anything else.

When Elizabeth finally emerged from her seminar, it was nearly five. The west side of the campus was quiet. Voices, music, and laughter wafted from the festival in the quad, but it seemed like a distant dream. She couldn't quite connect with it. Her head was too—too confused.

She hiked past the rock-climbing wall and recreation center toward the *Gazette* offices.

I have no idea what's in his head, Elizabeth thought miserably. *First he begs me to come back to the station. When I suggest it myself, I'm suddenly the invisible girlfriend.*

She gripped the strap of her pack and walked faster, the image of Tom's strange expression burning a hole in her heart. She'd always been able to read Tom so well. In fact, they'd often joked about how they could finish each other's sentences. Read each other's minds.

Elizabeth pushed open the door to the *Gazette* offices and hurried to her desk. Several reporters were bustling toward the coffee machine. Phones were ringing. Three sportswriters were gathered around a television set, watching a college basketball game.

"At least I have plenty to distract me," Elizabeth muttered, slipping into her desk chair. Though she'd worked for two hours that morning at the paper, she still had two minor campus stories she'd promised she'd bang out before the end of the day. After that she planned to catch an hour or two of studying in her room before her date that night with Tom at the beach.

A blinking light on her modem indicated an e-mail message. Elizabeth wearily logged on.

"Oh no." Elizabeth rested her forehead in her hand as she stared at the long message from Scott Sinclair on her screen. "Why won't he leave me alone?"

Hi, Elizabeth,
Knew you'd want the very first copy of my first published story in Colorado. It's a real groundbreaker, and I've got my fingers crossed for a big national journalism award.

"You must have the fattest head in Colorado now, Scott," Elizabeth muttered, scanning the article, which he'd cut and pasted in its entirety. "OK. Let's see what you've got. . . ."

HUNDREDS OF COLORADO UNIVERSITY
STUDENTS EXPELLED IN CREDIT FRAUD RING
BY SCOTT SINCLAIR AND EDIE MONROE
A network of more than three hundred Colorado students has been identified by federal investigators as one of the largest

credit card fraud rings in the country, according to . . .

"Nice work, Scott," Elizabeth murmured. "Too bad you're such an annoying egotist."

Elizabeth was just about to press the delete button when she glanced back at the byline at the top of the story. "Edie Monroe? Who's she?"

She gave the story another tired glance. With a quick keystroke she deleted it.

Chapter
Seven

"Direct from Los Angeles County, please welcome to the exclusive Alpha Chi house *Thirteen Stones!*"

Laughter and clapping rang through the fraternity's great hall, a vast, open space with a two-story vaulted ceiling. The balcony was strung with tiny white lights. Below, dozens of round tables were set up around the dance floor, each set with a glowing candle.

"Thank you, ladies and gentlemen," a guy with a subdued voice said over the PA.

Jessica looked up and felt her heart sink. *This* was the band everyone was so jazzed about? All she could see was four quiet, nerdy-looking guys in tacky tuxedos!

For a few awkward moments the four band members just stood quietly on the stage, looking out over the audience as if they didn't have a clue what to do next. Finally one of the band members sat down behind the drums. Then without warning he suddenly raised his drumsticks over his head and let out a loud, crazed howl. A split second later he burst into a drum solo.

Before Jessica realized it, the three other band members had peeled off their tuxedo jackets, white shirts, and ties, revealing ripped T-shirts. All at once they shook out their hair and tore into a song that was huge, wild, and irresistible.

"Yow!" Jessica shouted as everyone in Alpha Chi house went crazy.

"*Yeah!*" Isabella screamed. "Rock out, baby!"

The room shook with applause. Jessica jumped up from the table. Grabbing Nick by the hand, she plunged onto the crowded dance floor.

"These guys are hot!" she yelled as she shimmied toward the band.

Nick grinned. He was clapping and rocking his shoulders to the music, looking more handsome than she'd ever seen him. The smooth skin of his freshly shaven face gleamed against the white of his dress shirt. His dark hair was trimmed short, but after a few minutes of dancing a few sexy strands had fallen over his eyes, tempting Jessica to pull him close and brush them away.

Jessica glanced across the sea of bodies and checked for familiar faces. Lila Fowler was wearing an emerald green cocktail dress that showed off her loose, brunette hair, while her boyfriend, Bruce Patman, roamed the crowd in a perfectly tailored dark suit.

Alison Quinn sat sipping a glass of punch with her date at a nearby table. Jessica had to bite back giggles. The guy was almost an exact copy of Alison herself, from his stiff-backed posture to the superior way he looked down at the younger pledges who drew near to pay homage.

"Jessica! What a party, huh?" Denise shouted from the edge of the dance floor. She was sipping a beer and wearing a short black velvet dress. A silver clip glimmered in her hair. Her boyfriend, Winston Egbert, was on the dance floor, endangering the lives of nearby partygoers with a spastic break dance. The thick crowd had parted around him to cheer.

"Go, Winston! Go, Winston!" everyone chanted as Winston flopped onto his back, wrapped his long arms around his bony legs, and spun around like a curly-headed top.

"And what do we have here?" Jessica murmured as she turned to review the other side of the dance floor. She smiled. Isabella, in a formfitting black satin cocktail dress, was dancing directly in front of the band, her arms flailing wildly over her head.

She knew that Isabella liked to dance. But she'd never seen her cut loose like this before. Jessica choked back a giggle. Isabella looked especially wild dancing next to Danny. Wearing a boxy suit and a tortured look, Danny looked as if he were ready to bolt at any minute.

"Come on!" Jessica guided Nick closer to Isabella.

Danny gave Jessica a grim look, and he punched Nick lightly on the arm.

Isabella spun around and shimmied when she caught Jessica's eye. "Great party!"

"Yeah!" Jessica shouted. She stared in amazement as Isabella bent backward until her black hair swept the shiny dance floor. Danny quickly reached over to pull her up.

A few minutes later the band finished its number and began a slow one. Nick pulled Jessica close and laced his fingers into hers. Along the sidelines people wove in and out, munching on hors d'oeuvres and sipping from plastic cups.

Out of the corner of her eye Jessica saw a face she never would have expected in the exclusive Alpha Chi house. She squinted. Was that really Clay DiPalma?

What's he doing here?

Jessica watched Clay as he moved along the rim of the dance floor. He looked good in his gray double-breasted suit and silk tie, but he had a raw, unfinished quality to him that made him stand out from the rest of the fresh-faced frat boys.

Jessica felt a shiver. Clay's dark, dangerous eyes seemed to be taking everything and everyone in, as if he were memorizing it for future reference. His long hair was pulled back into a smooth ponytail, emphasizing his wide cheekbones and full lips. Jessica's eyes widened. She could just make out a dark red bruise on the left side of his face.

"Jessica?" Nick murmured into her ear. He leaned down and brushed his lips with hers. "Are you having a good time?"

"Yes," Jessica said, standing on tiptoe to whisper in his ear. Had Nick spotted Clay yet? The idea of a confrontation in front of SVU's entire Greek population did *not* appeal to her.

Nick spun her around. And Clay was looking straight at her.

For a split second Jessica felt herself reacting to

Clay's smoky stare. But as she pressed herself into Nick's chest and the music swelled, she realized that the sensation had already vaporized. Who needed Clay DiPalma? The hottest, sexiest, most dangerous man on earth was already there in her arms.

"Let's sit down." Danny motioned toward a table at the edge of the Alpha Chi dance floor.

Isabella shook her head and smiled. "Come on. This band is great!"

"No," Danny insisted, his expression turning serious. He suddenly stopped dancing, his body stiff and statuelike in the midst of hundreds of bouncing, flailing bodies.

Isabella cupped her hands around her mouth and yelled, "What's wrong?"

Danny glared at her and tried to grab her hand. "Come on."

Isabella shook her head. "Dance with me. It will help you relax!"

He leaned forward and yelled into her ear, "I'm not in the mood, Isabella."

"Well, *I* am."

For a moment Danny just stood there, his face like granite. Then he turned and disappeared into the crowd.

Isabella didn't follow. The music picked up again, and she kept dancing by herself, her arms and legs looser and freer than ever. Her shoes pinched her toes, and she stopped just long enough to pull them off. Her stockinged feet felt good against the slippery floor, and her long hair swooshed pleasantly against her shoulders.

She spun around, her head fizzing with a strange feeling of freedom. She closed her eyes, then opened them, her vision gradually focusing on an unfamiliar face in the dim light. She felt a peculiar tickle run up her spine. It was the face of a guy she'd never seen before, which was unusual for a party on Greek Row, where everybody knew everybody else.

Isabella moved closer, still dancing to the music, but taking in the olive skin and the direct, melting brown eyes that seemed to swallow her up.

He looked intently at her. Then just as quickly as he appeared, he turned away and faded into the crowd.

"Do I have any lipstick left? I forgot to take mine."

"Your lips have totally disappeared, Becky."

"Back off!"

"You can borrow mine."

"Why isn't this line moving?"

Jessica groaned. The spacious Alpha Chi house had only one smallish bathroom for women, and a line was already winding down the hallway. Precious party minutes were slipping away.

"May I?"

Jessica turned and grinned at Isabella's flushed face. "Isabella, you're cutting," she breathed. She gave the rest of the line a sly look, then pulled her friend in by the arm.

Isabella laughed. One black spaghetti strap slipped off her shoulder. "Don't tell anyone."

Jessica hooked her finger under the strap and

put it back in place. "*You're* having a good time," she drawled.

Isabella shook her head and caught her breath. "I guess."

Jessica narrowed her eyes. "OK. Spill."

"Spill what?" Isabella said, her gray eyes mysterious.

Jessica crossed her arms. "Actually, you could spill everything you and Danny Wyatt were up to these days and I'd end up with an empty glass."

"Who says I'm talking about Danny?" Isabella looked innocently up at the ceiling.

Jessica laughed. "Get outta here! I'm just kidding. You guys are stuck together like Super Glue."

Isabella looked down and groped all over her dress. "No glue here."

"Mmm," Jessica remarked. "No Danny nearby either. What's the matter? Did he have to go study for a calculus exam?"

Isabella rolled her eyes as the line inched forward. "No. He's still here, brooding over by Alpha Chi's trophy display."

"Whew. He's so baaad, that Danny."

Isabella's face suddenly turned serious. She heaved a big sigh. Jessica thought she'd never seen her face so pained. "You know, Jessica, I really love Danny."

"Yeah, but it sounds like trouble."

Isabella seemed to shake off her mood. In an instant her eyes brightened and her face broke into an enigmatic smile. "Actually, I don't want to talk about it," she said quickly, moving ahead with the line. "I just want to have a good time tonight."

Jessica high-fived her. "All right."

"And," Isabella whispered with a knowing smile, "I just saw the cutest guy out there. I've never seen him before at any of the frat parties."

"What's he look like?"

Isabella leaned closer. "Dark. Tall. Long hair. These big brown eyes you could fall into . . ."

Jessica groaned. "Oh yeah."

"Yeah, what?" Isabella asked.

"Yeah, like, that's Clay DiPalma."

"Do you know him?"

Jessica slid her fingers up the back of her neck and fluffed out her hair. "Well, let's just say he introduced himself to me the other day."

"He's completely hot." Isabella laughed and fanned her face. "Who is he?"

Jessica shrugged. "Who cares?"

"Jessica, you are too much."

"Yeah, well, I already have a boyfriend, remember?" Jessica giggled. "Sometimes Nick has to remind me of this, actually."

"Danny is *always* reminding me."

"Good for him," Jessica remarked, "especially when there are guys like Clay wandering around, undressing us with their eyes."

"Things are pretty tight with you and Nick, aren't they?" Isabella asked with a nudge.

Jessica suddenly felt a flood of warmth and pride. She nodded. "Yeah, if you can believe it."

"I can," Isabella said softly. There was a lull in the music, and Jessica detected the emotion in Isabella's voice. They squeezed into position just outside the ladies' room.

"Isn't Danny having a good time tonight?" Jessica prompted.

Isabella's face seemed to fold. "He has a hard time with that."

Jessica nodded and looked down.

"Things with me and Danny," Isabella went on, "well, I'm just not sure anymore. I don't know what's happened to him, but if he's not careful, I . . ."

"You'll what?"

"I just might go *look* for Clay DiPalma."

Jessica shook her finger. "Naughty, naughty."

"What were you two doing in there?" Nick asked impatiently once Jessica had emerged from the bathroom.

"None of your business," Jessica snapped. "Besides, it took us two hours to get in there, so how about a little sympathy?"

"Yeah, Nick," Isabella agreed, smoothing down her dress.

"Look," Nick said, drawing Jessica close as they threaded their way through the chaos. "There's just something I want to point out to you." He looked over at Isabella. "Hey, you too. Really."

Jessica exchanged glances with Isabella. Then she plucked a celery stick off an hors d'oeuvres tray. "What?"

"Yeah, what?" Isabella said.

"That guy."

Jessica stared down at her feet. Actually, she had known exactly what Nick was going to say. She'd seen it in his strained expression. She'd seen it in the way he rubbed the back of his neck. Nick had seen Clay DiPalma, and he was going ballistic.

"Oh, him," Jessica said, trying to sound casual. She looked across the room. Sure enough, there was Clay, drinking a bottle of beer and scanning the crowd.

"Stay away from him, Jess," Nick warned.

"Oh, stop it," Jessica complained.

"Stay away from whom?" Isabella asked.

Jessica turned to Isabella. "Clay DiPalma," she said in a low voice. "That studly creature you were asking about just a few minutes ago."

Nick raked his fingers through his hair. "Look, Isabella. Watch out for that guy. I don't have a good feeling about him."

"I guess that's why Nick punched him in the jaw when he tried to talk to me," Jessica murmured.

Isabella's eyes glittered. "Oooh, he did?"

"Be careful, OK, Isabella?" Nick asked.

Isabella turned away. "Gotta run. Bye, Ossifer!"

Nick glowered. "Jessica, I—"

"You've made your point, Nick." Jessica put her hands on her hips. "You say you don't want to be a cop anymore, but look at yourself. Detective Nick Fox is back."

"He's trouble, Jess. I just want to make sure you understand."

Jessica narrowed her eyes. "Are you telling me who I can talk to? Who I can *handle*?"

"Jess, don't—"

"You're not my father!" Jessica pouted. "I can make

my own decisions. What's going on with you anyway?"

"That guy . . . what's his name?"

"Clay DiPalma," Jessica said, her voice rising with irritation. "Clay DiPalma. Clay DiPalma. He's not the first guy in the world who's ever flirted with me. What's the big *deal?*"

"Calm down."

"I'm sorry, Nick, but sometimes I wonder if you've seen a teensy-weensy bit too much violence, crime, and gore. It's made you paranoid." Jessica held up her hand as Nick opened his mouth. "To you, everyone's a suspect. To me, everyone is innocent until proven guilty."

Jessica turned away and rolled her eyes. Just as she was about to check out the action on the dance floor, she heard a soft chuckle right behind her. She looked up and caught her breath. There, within earshot, was Clay DiPalma himself. He was staring—staring and laughing.

She bit her bottom lip. The whole situation was starting to get seriously hilarious. A part of her wanted to laugh right along with Clay, but she didn't want to hurt Nick's feelings.

"What are you looking at?" Nick said sharply.

"Stop it," Jessica whispered. She nudged Nick with her hip and covered her mouth.

For a moment Clay just stood there, smiling out of the corner of his mouth and eyeing Nick. Then without a word he turned and disappeared into the throng.

Danny Wyatt really did have incredible powers of discipline. He prided himself on being able to focus entirely on the task at hand. It didn't matter what it was. Math. Wrestling. Fixing an electrical outlet. Making a cheesecake. Controlling his temper. To him, it was all pretty much the same.

"Except for dancing, maybe. I can't focus on that," Danny muttered to himself as he strolled past the Alpha Chis' impressive trophy displays. He'd left the dance floor only a few minutes ago just to get away from the blasting music and laughter. The high-pitched buzz in his left ear was driving him crazy.

And I can focus on Isabella just great, Danny thought miserably. *But it doesn't work the other way around—I can see that right now.*

Danny sighed as he strolled past a couple wrapped in a passionate embrace next to the coat closet. Isabella was a person, after all: beautiful, unpredictable, and with a mind of her own. He wasn't sure he understood what was going on inside that mind. Not anymore.

She seemed so restless and distracted these days. It seemed, in fact, that every time he looked at her, she was looking the other way. Was it him? Was she getting tired of him? Worse, could she be in love with someone else?

Danny suddenly felt as if he'd been punched in the stomach. He stopped and struggled to think.

When did the change begin? Yesterday? Two weeks ago? A month? Was it something I said? Something I forgot to say? Is there a law in nature that says a love like this can't last forever? Does it just slow down and then flicker out? Or can you breathe life back into it before it's too late?

He turned and hurried back down the hall toward

the dance floor, searching for a glimpse of Isabella. The night was still young, after all. He'd find her and dance with her—all night if she wanted to. He had to try.

He pushed past a redheaded girl who was giggling uncontrollably at a guy who was standing on his head near the punch bowl. Then he threaded his way through five guys in the midst of a beer-chugging contest.

Danny suddenly stopped on the edge of the dance floor. At that moment he thought he'd caught a glimpse of Isabella in the midst of the moving bodies, though he wasn't sure. And then he heard a wild, high-pitched laugh that sounded vaguely familiar.

He walked slowly along the edge of the dancers until he got right up to the front, near the band. In the midst of the bobbing heads he could barely make out Isabella's face. He drew closer still, then stopped and felt his face grow hot with anger.

There, in the middle of the crowd, was Isabella. Her head was thrown back, her gray eyes were flashing, and her hips were swinging in a wild, back-and-forth motion.

Isabella wasn't dancing alone anymore. She was dancing with three other guys. Danny's fists tightened with each swing of Isabella's hips.

"Isabella!" he shouted, shoving the crowd aside with his powerful arms. "Come on. We're getting out of here."

Isabella's dancing slowed, and she looked at him with alarm. "Stop it, Danny."

Danny grabbed her arm and began dragging her off.

"Get away!" Isabella yelled.

"Let go of her," one of the guys shouted.

Danny tightened his grip on her arm and pulled her toward the front entry.

"What are you *doing?*" Isabella shouted angrily, yanking her arm away. "You're hurting me."

"I can't take this anymore," Danny said, wiping the sweat off his forehead with the back of his hand.

"I will not leave," Isabella said indignantly. "And I wouldn't leave with you even if I *wanted* to. What makes you think you can just haul me away like some kind of . . . *possession?*"

Danny felt his pulse race with fury. "I wouldn't have to do this if you could control yourself a little."

"Give me a *break*."

"How many guys were you dancing with at once? Three? Four?" Danny growled, ignoring the stares of the partygoers flooding in and out of the front door.

Isabella yanked her spaghetti straps back onto her shoulders and smoothed her hair. "I'm having fun. Have you ever heard of that word? *Fun?* It's a really great concept, Danny. Especially when you need to work off a little steam, like I do. . . ."

"You looked like a maniac out there," Danny said. "Are you that desperate for attention?"

Isabella's eyes were on fire. "I wouldn't need any attention at all if my so-called boyfriend weren't wandering around this party like a ghost."

"Like a what?"

"You took me to a dance, and now you refuse to dance with me," Isabella argued. "What am I supposed to do?"

"I didn't even *want* to come."

"Then why did you?"

"Because I wanted to protect you!"

"Protect me from *what?*"

Danny grabbed Isabella's bare shoulders and shook them. "Protect you from yourself!"

"Let go!"

"You're acting . . . so different," Danny struggled. "I'm—I'm worried. I don't want you to—do anything you'll regret!"

"Regret?" Isabella shouted. She shook off his hands and stepped away. Her face was pink, and Danny could see tiny beads of perspiration on her upper lip. "Regret?"

Danny held up his hands.

"What was that supposed to mean?" Isabella demanded.

Danny shook his head. He wished he hadn't said quite so much. "You—you don't understand. . . ."

"Oh yes, I do," Isabella said in a stony voice. "Something I'll regret, huh?"

"Isabella—"

"You ain't seen nothing yet, Danny," Isabella warned. "You just watch. You just watch and see how much fun I can have tonight. And I promise you, Danny Wyatt, I will never regret it. Not for a second."

Chapter Eight

"OK," Tom began. "You want the deluxe burger. Hold the pickles. Extra sauce. French fries on the side. Diet Coke."

Elizabeth leaned back into the restaurant's comfortable wooden chair, eyeing him skeptically. "Right."

"Of course I'm right."

"How did you know?"

Tom shrugged. "I just know. I just know *you*."

Elizabeth shook her head and smiled. "Is this a good thing?"

"What thing?" Tom asked.

"That we know each other so well."

Tom looked thoughtful. "OK. This is a test. What am *I* going to order?"

Elizabeth pressed her lips together and thought. "The special. You're interested in the special."

Tom's jaw dropped. "How did you know?"

"Because it's Saturday night. You always feel upbeat on Saturday nights. You're more prone to take

112

chances. To try new things." She grinned at him. "And you like corned beef."

Tom whistled. "This is scary."

Elizabeth sipped her water and took in her surroundings. It was an old-fashioned creek-side restaurant with red-and-white checked curtains, a crackling fire, and cheerful white-haired waitresses. A long counter ran along the other side of the room, and there were lots of busy tables in between, filled with a mix of college students and families.

"One more thing," Elizabeth said, trying to suppress her smile. "You're planning to ask for an extra pickle."

Tom balled up his paper napkin and threw it at her. "No, I'm not."

"Liar." Elizabeth snaked her foot around Tom's ankle.

Tom shook his foot. "Help! The truth has trapped me. It's sucking me down. It's squeezing me!"

Elizabeth laughed and fiddled with the edges of her menu. "It's good to get off campus for a while."

Tom drew his eyebrows together. "How come? What's going on?"

Elizabeth hesitated. "Oh . . . stuff."

"Hmmm," Tom teased. "Folks down at the *Gazette* have a secret they don't want to spill to their friends over at WSVU, huh?" He eagerly folded his hands in front of him and lifted one eyebrow. "Come on. Trying to scoop us? Fat chance."

Elizabeth let out a short laugh.

"Hey. What's wrong?"

Elizabeth cupped her chin in her hands and looked into his eyes. "Hey, it's nothing like that. But I mean—I don't really know if this is the right time to bring it up."

Tom's expression softened. "Bring what up?"

Elizabeth bit her lip. "Um. Well, it has to do with Scott Sinclair."

Tom suddenly leaned back in his chair and averted his eyes. "Oh, man."

"Hey," Elizabeth said softly. "We don't have to talk about this if it's going to wreck our evening." She paused. "But I don't think we should always avoid the subject of—you know—who we dated—"

"OK," Tom interrupted, holding up his hands.

Elizabeth straightened. "Look. I don't want to dwell on Scott. But I don't want to avoid the subject when it comes up either."

"So what happened?" Tom asked quietly.

"He keeps trying to contact me," Elizabeth told him. "It's so weird. He's been sending me stuff at the *Gazette,* as if I'm really interested in the daily progress he's making toward his inevitable Pulitzer Prize."

Tom looked relieved when the waitress approached. And when he and Elizabeth were done placing their orders, Elizabeth noticed he wasn't too eager to get back to the subject of Scott Sinclair.

"Anyway," Elizabeth prompted, playing with her fork and knife. "That's what's going on with me, I guess."

For a second Tom looked as if he were going to ignore her statement. But then he suddenly leaned forward and lowered his voice. "What did you ever see in that guy?"

Elizabeth drew back, instantly sorry she'd ever broached the subject. She'd been longing for Tom's sympathy and support. But Tom was obviously *not* willing to be charitable when it came to matters involving Scott Sinclair.

She took a deep breath. "What did I see in Scott Sinclair," she echoed. "Um. Ambition? Yes, I definitely saw ambition."

Tom seemed to relax. "You can do better than that."

"Um. Blue eyes? Flattery?" Elizabeth continued. "An easy ticket out of Sweet Valley?"

Tom shook his head.

Actually, Elizabeth wished she didn't have to merely joke around about Scott. She wanted to explain the deep attraction she'd had to Scott—like, for example, the way she admired his take-charge attitude. And the way she felt invincible with him, as if he had his hands on the controls and could take the two of them anywhere they wanted to go.

Plus, Elizabeth thought with a pang, *Scott was a way of getting back at you, Tom, in case you haven't figured that out. It wasn't easy watching you flaunt Dana Upshaw all over campus.*

Tom was giving her a serious look. But it seemed to her that he was very, very distant, as if he were thinking about something else altogether.

"The thing with Scott just happened, I guess," Elizabeth murmured. She looked up and blushed.

"No. I mean, *nothing* happened, actually."

Tom looked down. "Oh."

Elizabeth slipped her fingers into Tom's hand. "You know what I mean."

Tom shrugged.

"Hey." Elizabeth tried to look into his eyes, but they were focused somewhere near her right shoulder. "You and I weren't apart for *that* long. I mean, how much can happen in that short a time?"

Tom cleared his throat, withdrew his hand, and scratched the back of his neck.

"Anyway," Elizabeth went on, "Scott is gone now. And I hope I never see him again in my life. . . ."

"Yeah," Tom said, tapping a finger on his fork. The waitress sailed by with a platter of steaks. Elizabeth could hear the man at the next table asking for A1 sauce.

"Tom? Is there something wrong?"

"Huh? Oh no. No, I'm fine."

Elizabeth felt a little queasy inside. Bringing up the subject of Scott had definitely dampened the mood. She searched her mind for something to say.

"So," Elizabeth said without thinking. "Do you—um—keep in touch with Dana?" As soon as the words came out of her mouth, she regretted them.

Tom cleared his throat. "Uh—no."

Elizabeth shrugged. "You're not even friends?"

Tom shook his head. "No big deal."

"She . . . she didn't seem like your type," Elizabeth said gently. She followed up with a short chuckle. "A little wacky for you, actually . . ."

116

Tom coughed loudly. "Yeah, well, it wasn't that serious. Hey, have we ordered yet?"

Elizabeth looked at him skeptically. "Yes, Tom. We did."

"Oh."

Elizabeth pulled at her ponytail. She knew Tom could be the most straightforward, honest guy in the world when he wanted to be. So why did he have to get so nervous when she mentioned Dana? Couldn't they just talk about it and move on?

Why was it such a big deal?

Isabella's cheeks were burning as she stomped away from Danny and headed straight for the dance floor. The band had just punched into a pulsating beat. Everyone was jumping up from the tables to dance.

Swinging her bare arms, she danced straight into the crowd, desperate to drown herself in the music and lights. She danced past the welcoming committee table, the stage, and the limbo contest. She danced around the punch bowl table and shimmied together with several Thetas in the middle of the dance floor.

Gasping for breath, Isabella finally stopped and leaned up against one of Alpha Chi's fancy indoor columns. She was dizzy. Her throat was parched. She realized that she hadn't eaten anything in hours.

"Hi."

Isabella turned and looked at a guy in a blue blazer and tie. Swaying slightly, he offered her a small silver flask he'd drawn from his inside jacket pocket.

"Mmm." Isabella took the flask, put it to her

117

mouth, and tipped it up. Though the liquor tasted strong and bitter, Isabella drank it thirstily, letting its hot warmth trickle down her throat and chest. A few moments later she felt a pleasant, tingling sensation course through her body. She took another long drink and slipped the flask back into the guy's jacket, patting his pocket in silent thanks.

"Uh-huh," the guy said.

Isabella slipped away into the crowd, enjoying her newly relaxed, loose-limbed feeling. All she wanted to do was throw herself into the mass of bodies. To completely wipe Danny from her mind. If an ocean cliff had presented itself, Isabella was sure she would have happily jumped off it—just to show him how much she didn't care.

"Watch where you're going!"

"Eek!" Isabella caught her heel in the crack of the wooden floor and nearly crashed into a group of girls ladling punch into plastic cups.

"Sorry!" Isabella sang out, closing her eyes and spinning off in the opposite direction. A few moments later she opened her eyes as a warm, happy thought began to snake its way through her mind.

Clay DiPalma.

Isabella hugged herself. That was his name, wasn't it? Clay DiPalma. Of course. He was the kind of person she was in the mood to hang out with. The very thought of him sent shivers up her back. But where was he now?

"Hi, Isabella!"

Isabella turned and realized she was standing a

mere foot from a table jam-packed with some of her closest friends. Lila was parked on Bruce's lap, sipping champagne. Jessica was snuggled next to her boyfriend, Nick Fox. Denise and Winston were singing along with the band.

"Isabella?"

It took Isabella a few moments to realize that Lila was talking to her. "Yes?" she said slowly.

Lila watched as Bruce poured champagne into her glass. Then she looked back up at Isabella with a matter-of-fact expression. "Where's Danny?"

"Danny?" Isabella barely met her eyes. "I don't know."

"Is Izzy looking for Danny?" Winston asked spacily.

Denise rumpled Winston's hair. "Duh! Who else would she be looking for?"

Isabella looked at the group in confusion and tried to slip by them.

"I saw Danny by the trophy display!" Winston yelled.

"*Izzy!* What's up?"

Isabella whirled around and squinted. Jessica was now trailing her. "Come sit with us," Jessica urged. "Danny will be able to find you there."

Isabella gritted her teeth and pushed past Jessica. She rushed into a small pocket of space on the dance floor, took a deep breath, and began dancing again. Somehow Jessica disappeared into the dim, swirling lights, and Isabella found herself blissfully alone—in a room filled with hundreds of people.

"Hi."

Isabella felt warm breath in her ear. She turned, half expecting to see the impossible. She closed her eyes. Then a moment later she opened them again and felt a deep thrill. There they were again. The bottomless brown eyes. The thick brown hair. The full mouth that seemed to beckon her forward.

"Hi," Isabella finally said.

Clay DiPalma gave her a sexy, crooked smile. His face had paled slightly and his tie was loose, but his eyes took her in hungrily, as if he'd been searching for her all night. Though they'd barely spoken, Isabella found herself swaying with him to the music. He slipped his arm around her waist and pulled her in. "I'm Clay."

"Isabella," she said. There was a warm, tingling sensation on her hip, where Clay's hand rested. His shirtfront grazed her chest, and Isabella had to tighten her grip on his neck to keep from buckling. What was it about this guy that was making her so dizzy? Was it the self-assured, almost taunting look in his eyes? The lips that made her want to . . .

"Would you like to dance, Isabella?" he whispered.

She felt his breath in her ear and shivered. His hand slipped boldly around her waist, and she could feel his warmth against her. "OK," she said. For a moment she was sure that her body was actually melting into his.

Clay led her near the center of the floor, and almost as soon as he did, the music slowed. Isabella closed her eyes while Clay slipped one hand farther down her back and held her firmly. He moved in even closer, pressing his other hand into Isabella's palm, then spreading his fingers and lacing them tightly into hers.

Isabella tipped back her head and stared at him, unafraid. Somewhere in the back of her mind, there was Danny. But it wasn't hard to push the image away—not while she was drinking in the sight of Clay DiPalma.

"So . . . where's your boyfriend?"

"What boyfriend?"

Clay's smile broadened. "You're a real heart-breaker, huh?"

"You just watch me."

Clay winked. "That won't be too hard."

Isabella felt as if she were drowning in pleasure. Yet a part of her began to wonder what he was doing at a fraternity cocktail party. Clay was the kind of guy who looked as if he belonged in a recording studio or at an art gallery opening. He wasn't exactly the button-down type.

Still, Isabella didn't really want to ask. All she cared about was the crazy, wonderful way he was making her feel. She felt loosened. Free. As if she could handle anything that came her way by herself and on her own terms.

"Hey, let's get out of here," Clay said after a few minutes. His mouth curled into a sexy smile, and he nodded toward the large French doors that led to the fraternity's porch and garden. "I need a smoke."

Isabella accepted his hand and followed him out through the noisy crowd.

"Cigarette?" Clay said softly. He leaned against the doorjamb and shook out the pack he'd drawn out of his inside coat pocket.

Isabella hesitated. She'd only tried smoking a few times in her life and had hated it. If she tried it again now, there was a chance she'd start gagging or worse. Still, she couldn't help smiling at the thought of Danny's face if he ever saw her puffing away. Danny was the kind of health nut who worshiped the food pyramid and worried the cafeteria wasn't using enough organically grown vegetables in its salad bar. But cigarette smoking? To Danny, cigarette smoking was utterly rock-bottom, criminal behavior he hoped would someday be punishable by life in prison, deportation, or death by lethal injection.

"Come on," Clay urged her. "It won't bite you."

"Yeah, I know," Isabella said smoothly. She took a cigarette, slipped it expertly between two fingers, and put it to her lips.

Clay drew a lighter out of his pants pocket and lit her cigarette. Then he carefully took a second cigarette from the pack and lit it for himself.

Isabella pulled on the cigarette and watched it glow. She inhaled the smoke, then blew it out in a thin stream, praying she wouldn't choke.

"I've been watching you all night," Clay began, taking a long drag and blowing his smoke out languidly. "Where do you live?"

Isabella closed her eyes halfway and gave him a long look. "Why do you want to know?"

"Because I want to see you again."

"I see." Isabella took another drag of her cigarette.

Clay flicked his cigarette ash out the door. "Are you cool with that?"

Isabella said nothing.

Clay chuckled and flicked his eyes toward the Theta table. "Whoa. Is this OK right now? I mean, are the sorority party police going to come and take you away for talking to me?"

Isabella gave him her most mysterious smile. When she turned to blow out her smoke, she suddenly caught a glimpse of Danny lingering near the front door, his mouth open in shock. Her head began to throb and her stomach felt sick, but before she could really think about what she was doing, she gave him a defiant look and took another long drag.

At first Danny just stood there, his lips pressed together as if he could barely contain his rage. He shook his head and walked quickly out the door.

Stop, she wanted to call out to him. *I want to know what's happening to us. I'm afraid!*

Still, when Isabella looked back at Clay, she found it was easier to fight off her worries. Maybe Clay showed up at the perfect time. Maybe her attraction to Clay would help her understand how terribly wrong things were with Danny.

Where had the fun gone? The passion? Why did she have to blame herself for everything that went wrong between them?

Isabella pulled deeply on her cigarette and threw back her head defiantly. Danny was the one who decided to have a lousy time tonight, not her. And if she got swept off her feet by this exciting, totally thrilling guy standing right next to her, then good for her! Danny was just going to have to deal with it.

Danny deserved everything he got, she decided. If he didn't learn to loosen up, he was going to lose her for good.

"Now *that* was a burger," Elizabeth said. She dabbed the corners of her mouth with her red-checked napkin.

"It's in the sauce," Tom said mysteriously. "Something no one can explain."

Elizabeth laughed. "Now you tell me."

"The Creekside Inn's top secret recipe," Tom explained. "WSVU tried to investigate about a month ago, but we couldn't crack Mrs. Murphy's recipe box." Tom smiled. "She locks it up at night."

Elizabeth's laugh rang out, and her cheeks flushed a very delicate pink. Tom cupped the side of his face in one hand and gazed at her. What was that color, he wondered dreamily. Sometimes he thought it was the pink of the very first signs of sunset over the Pacific. Other times it was the very pale pink on the inside of a seashell. The pink of a rose . . .

"Anyway," Elizabeth said carefully, stirring her Coke with a straw. "Thanks for dinner. I'm sorry I brought up the subject of—you know—"

Tom's face fell. "Looks like you just brought it up again."

Elizabeth looked back. "Sorry." She paused. "I guess."

"Don't worry about it."

"I'm not *worried*," Elizabeth explained as the waitress took her plate away. "I was just thinking out loud."

"Oh."

"Maybe I just need to talk about what happened—you know—after we broke up," Elizabeth went on. "After all, it was a pretty confusing time."

Tom felt his stomach tighten.

"I'm still confused in a way," Elizabeth explained. She began playing nervously with the paper napkin in front of her. "I mean, I really don't know what I saw in Scott Sinclair. What was I doing anyway? Now that I look back on it, I know I didn't really feel that much for him at all. It was never anything close to what we had—what we have."

Tom felt his heart drop into his gut.

"It only made me miss you more than ever." Elizabeth gave him a shy look. "We could talk about this. Or—I guess we could drop it."

"I'm leaning toward dropping it."

"Oh, OK." Elizabeth sighed. "I'm sorry. I didn't mean to—"

"No. Really. Stop," Tom said, waving one hand in front of him. "It's OK. Let's just talk about something else."

Elizabeth bit her bottom lip and nodded silently.

Tom shifted in his seat. Elizabeth's face was so beautiful, yet so sad and strained. He knew how important honesty was to her. Yet there was just no way he could open up right now. It was just too hard.

Elizabeth's eyes were damp and confused. "Are you done?"

"Yeah," Tom whispered. "I mean, no."

"No?" Elizabeth said, looking at his plate. "You've eaten every last crumb."

"I know," Tom grumbled. There was so much he wanted to tell her. He wanted to be at peace with Elizabeth, and yet—"I just . . ."

"You just what?"

"I just . . ."

Elizabeth's smile widened, and her whole face seemed to light up with love. Love shimmered off her blond hair and glowed in her eyes. Tom thought about how much he needed her, and how in an instant everything they had together could disappear.

"You just *what?*" Elizabeth laughed, taking his hand.

Tom realized that he had stopped breathing. He dropped his shoulders in defeat and sucked in a lungful of air. "I just loved that corned beef sandwich."

Elizabeth laughed again. "I think it gave you a stomachache. You should see the look on your face. You look green."

Tom laughed too, relieved that the moment had passed. Nothing had changed between them.

He didn't care if he went crazy holding it inside of him, even if he had to do it forever.

He loved Elizabeth too much to hurt her.

"Look at that guy over there." Jessica gasped. "He just did a handspring across the dance floor. Yow."

Lila flipped back a wedge of her chestnut hair. "He's a Sig. Just won the NCAA regional gymnastics meet. He does that every time he sees a smooth, shiny surface."

Jessica and Lila had pushed their chairs together at the far end of the Theta table and were nibbling on the late night party fare the Alpha Chis had just brought out.

"I bet Nick could do a handspring," Jessica said with a sigh.

"Yeah," Lila agreed. "They probably taught them that in the police academy."

Jessica and Lila looked at each other, then burst out laughing.

Jessica rolled her eyes and bit into a small sandwich. "It'll never happen. Nick's into caution right now."

Lila nudged her and rolled her chunky gold bracelets up and down her arm. "Come on, Jess. Nick is perfect for you, and you know it." She glanced toward a cluster of frat guys gathered around Nick near the punch bowl. "Plus he's totally hot. Check out the way those guys are circling him like he's Mr. Alpha Stud of the wolf pack. He's probably telling them another killer True Story of the Highway Patrol."

"Yeah."

"Look at the way they're watching him," Lila said, grabbing Jessica's wrist. "And look at Bruce go gaga."

Jessica spotted Bruce and nodded.

Lila was laughing. "Looks like Bruce is going to launch into a hot story of his own to match Nick's. Look at him! He's swelling out his chest for effect."

Jessica took a sip of champagne and giggled.

"The closest Bruce has ever come to the underworld was the time that guy in Florida used his identity to get a Visa card." Lila snorted.

Jessica giggled. "I remember now. He was totally insulted when he got a bill for a suit and tie from Kmart."

"He wouldn't have noticed if it had come from Brooks Brothers or Saks," Lila said with a sigh, her glance roaming back toward Nick. "Now Nick, on the other hand . . ."

Jessica slapped her thigh. "Oh yeah. He would have jumped all over that guy. Both stun guns going off at once. Handcuffs. Warrants. You name it."

Lila lifted one eyebrow. "What a man."

"I guess."

"What do you mean by that?"

"He's Mr. Superman," Jessica explained, picking up a stuffed pastry shell. "What can I say? He wants to save everyone, especially Jessica Wakefield."

"Stop scarfing those things," Lila scolded, yanking the plate away. "Jeez. Nick *is* getting on your nerves. Your high-fat intake always skyrockets when your men give you trouble."

Jessica crossed her legs. "Don't get me wrong. I'm crazy about Nick. But he's always getting on my case about *what* I'm doing and *who* I'm talking to and *how* dangerous everything is."

"Get out. I thought he was Mr. Excitement."

"No," Jessica explained. "He's already *seen* plenty of excitement. Now he wants to *avoid* it."

"Bor-ing." Lila sighed. She looked away. Then she sat abruptly upright. "Hey. Check this out, Jess."

"What?" Jessica grabbed another hors d'oeuvre as soon as Lila looked away.

"Isabella," Lila said in a wondering voice. She stood up. "Isabella looks like she's . . . sort of . . . *drunk*."

"Impossible," Jessica exclaimed, swallowing quickly. "Isabella is too classy for that. I think she had half a glass of wine, max."

"Well, look at her."

Jessica squinted. "Oooh. No wonder Danny took off. She's with Clay DiPalma."

Lila drew herself up. "Who's Clay DiPalma? *I've* never heard of him in my life."

"Well, where have you been, Lila Fowler?"

Lila gave her an impatient look. "Spill."

Jessica leaned closer. "He's this totally hot guy I talked to this week. . . ."

"He looks a little rough around the edges to me," Lila said, putting a hand on her hip. "And look at the way he's sort of smiling at Isabella, like she just said something totally funny."

Jessica continued to watch, first Isabella, then Clay. Lila was right. Clay *was* a little rough around the edges. Somehow she could see that better now that he wasn't so up close. She narrowed her eyes. What was Isabella up to?

"Lila?" Jessica grabbed Lila's wrist.

"What?"

"Isabella doesn't look so good," Jessica said slowly. "There. See? She's really weaving."

"You're right," Lila said worriedly. "She's looks like she's about to fall over. And that guy seems to think it's totally funny!"

Jessica watched with growing alarm as Isabella finally put her hand on Clay's shoulder for balance. "Something's wrong," she murmured. "Something's really, really wrong."

At first Isabella felt strangely distant. She spoke, but her words disconnected from her brain. An odd, loose feeling came over her. Her head floated above her neck. Her limbs rose up on their own. She was slowly, slowly being filled with helium gas.

"What?" she heard herself ask.

Clay's mouth, inches away, moved. But the sound that came out wasn't familiar. His forehead swelled slightly, then shrank.

She shook her head. "What?"

"Isabella? Isabella? Isabella?" the sound echoed.

She reached out her hands for balance. The floor began to warp and buckle beneath her feet.

What was happening?

Someone took her hand as the room began to whirl. But there was no place to set her feet. The world had turned from solid to liquid. She was drowning. *I need a wall,* Isabella thought in desperation. She found one and pressed her palm against it, trying to focus.

Clay's face again. At first like an angel's, then suddenly twisted. His eyes flashed red. His hands were claws. They gripped her shoulders, hurting her.

"Get away!" someone shouted, long and low.

Moments later she realized it was her. Her hands pushed the sound away. The walls—so close. The ceiling—pressing down, nearly to the top of her head. The air—so thick. Was she underwater now? Could she breathe?

"Isabella? Isabella? Isabella?"

She pressed her hands to her cheeks. The echo. She had to shake it off.

"Isabella? Isabella? Isabella?"

Her feet began to move beneath her. Shapes and faces slipped quickly past. "No. I'm going. Now. No. Please."

"Isabella?"

She turned toward the claw that was now grasping her arm. Jessica? Why were her lips moving so strangely? And her nose. It was completely gone!

"Isabella?"

"Lila? Jessica?" she heard someone say. Was it her own voice? Or the voice of ghosts?

There were many faces now. Faces she knew and had once loved. Now they were angry with her. They surrounded her in the darkness and the whirling lights. Hands—everywhere—pinning her down. Eyes—glaring at her with hate.

"Stop," she screamed. She shook off the claws. Her heart hammered in her rib cage. Her skin crawled. "Get away. Get away."

The monsters chased her. She had to find a way out. She couldn't breathe. What was happening? Was she about to die? Was there time to break free and save herself?

"Isabella? What's wrong?"

She turned and saw Jessica's face—a wild beast's. Her eyes glittered. Fur bristled on her neck. She grasped the back of Isabella's dress.

"Leave me alone!" Isabella cried.

She stumbled forward to escape. The faces swarmed. All beasts now. Glittering eyes. Fangs. They flew past as she ran. They breathed in her air. A door. She needed to be outside. She must breathe!

"Isabella. Stop—stop—stop—stop!"

A staircase stretched out in front of her, long and sweeping. A river of air cascaded down. She could breathe up there. There was space too. Her legs took over. She headed up, two steps at a time. Sweat trickled down the front of her dress, scalding her.

"Isabella!" the beasts shrieked below. Hundreds of them. The eyes. The fangs. The sucking of air. *"Come here. Come here. Come here."*

"Get away!" she screamed. She was upstairs now. Her arms were wings now, flying faster than the beasts behind. "Leave me alone!"

To her side, she smelled it. There was a door, and the air rushed out. She spread her wings and banked into it. Life-giving air. She breathed. Life. The smell of grass and water and stars. She flew through the door into the dark room where the river of air began. Where she had to be.

Here it was—at last. Up ahead, a glass door opened to a balcony. White curtains stirred at the windows, calling her.

"Isabella—bella—bella—bella!"

She heard the snarls and shrieks of wild animals mounting the stairs behind her. She saw how much they wanted her. Their claws reached out to her, sharp as razors. They pressed toward her, all breathing in the precious air.

"Stop!" Isabella screamed. She stepped backward. She flailed her arms in front of her face to scare them. "Get away!"

"We—want—to—help—you."

Then in an instant Isabella felt the cool, tempting air at her back. It floated in through the window where the curtains fluttered so beautifully. All she had to do was turn and leave.

Now! she thought. She spread her wings wide and flew so high and fast. She circled joyfully over the screaming beasts below, safe from the claws that reached up to snag her.

"Good-bye!" she sang out to them.

Then she turned and picked up speed for her flight onto the balcony. Into the lovely wide-open darkness beyond.

Chapter
Nine

"*Isabella?*" Jessica cried.

"Oh, my God!" Lila screamed, running up to Jessica's side. "Where is she?"

Both had staggered to a stop at an open doorway on the top floor of the Alpha Chi house. Peering inside, they could see a disheveled bedroom that was quiet and dark except for the flicker of a computer screen and the stray beams of moonlight stirring in its open French door.

Jessica stepped forward, still trying to catch her breath. "Isabella? Where are you?"

"She was just in here," Lila sobbed. "I saw her go through this door!"

"Oh no," Jessica cried softly. She hurried toward the French door. There was a balcony beyond it that looked over the fraternity's backyard. Moments ago she had seen Isabella tear into this same room, screaming wildly, as if she were being chased by demons.

"*I-sa-bel-la!*" Lila suddenly wailed. "*Oh, please, no!*"

Jessica rushed through the cluttered room and stepped onto the narrow balcony that ran along the length of the house. The cool night air stirred against her face. She squinted into the darkness. "Isabella?" she cried softly, looking to her right and left. Nothing. She felt a clutch at her throat. Terrified, she stepped toward the railing and peered over.

"Is she there?" Lila screamed behind her. "Is she there? Why aren't you . . ."

"Isabella?" Jessica wailed. Her eyes dropped down, and her fear suddenly flipped into mind-numbing terror. Sprawled on the grass below was Isabella's motionless body. She was lying on her back. Her placid, chalk white face could be seen clearly in the midst of her tangled black hair.

"What happened?" Lila shrieked, stumbling onto the balcony next to Jessica and grabbing the railing.

"She fell!" Jessica cried. *"Isabella!"*

"Someone call an ambulance!" Lila yelled.

Jessica drew her hands up to her face in horror.

Tiny, hysterical shrieks began to emerge from Lila, followed by deep sobs, then high-pitched screams. Flailing her arms for balance, Lila turned on her heel and tottered back into the house.

"Is she . . . dead?" Jessica whispered, alone and paralyzed on the balcony.

"Help!" Lila screamed from inside the house.

"She can't be dead," Jessica said. A burst of panic surged through her body, and she turned on her heel. She staggered back into the room and dashed

135

for the stairs, her only thought to get to the ground, where Isabella lay alone in the cold darkness.

"Help!" Jessica screamed at the top of her lungs. She stumbled down the stairs and joined Lila, who was waving her arms over her head. "Stop the music! Please! Help!"

"What happened?" Bruce cried out. Denise dashed up behind him, along with dozens of other partygoers.

"Call nine-one-one," Jessica yelled. Wild tears sprang into her eyes as she pushed through the group and headed for the nearest door. "Come on!" she yelled over her shoulder. "It's Isabella. She . . . fell . . . over the balcony."

A gasp rose up from the crowd, and the music began to break up.

"She's on the ground on the other side of the house," Lila shouted. Her hands shook.

"Alison's calling now," Denise yelled.

"Come on!" Jessica yelled. She shoved open a side door. "We need help! Nick!"

"Jess!" Nick shouted. In a heartbeat he was at her side.

Jessica grabbed his steady hand and tore down a dimly lit stone path. It wove through a sloping lawn, which was dotted with flower beds and trees.

"There she is!" Nick called out as they sprinted across the grass. Up ahead, Jessica could see the shadowy outline of Isabella's still, awkward body collapsed near a bush on the grass. Lights flicked on at the back of the frat house, illuminating her deathly white face.

"Isabella!" Jessica cried out. She ran ahead and

136

knelt beside her friend. Her whole body went numb. Isabella's face was still. A deep, bloody cut ran across her forehead. Her right cheekbone had begun to swell horribly. "Isabella. Wake up!" Jessica stared at her in a wild panic. "Oh no, is she . . . ?"

"Don't *touch* her!" Nick shouted again. He knelt down and bent his head to Isabella's chest. "She's breathing, but she could have a serious spinal injury."

Jessica bit her bottom lip hard. Isabella's upturned right elbow was contorted at a ghastly angle. She could see the disconnected bone pressing up against the skin.

"An ambulance is coming!" someone called out in the darkness.

Jessica cupped her hands around her mouth and shouted, "Someone bring some blankets. Quick!"

"Izzy," Lila moaned softly. She knelt down next to Nick and Jessica.

"She's breathing," Jessica said in a cracked voice. She ran her hand helplessly down the side of Isabella's arm.

"I don't believe it," Lila sobbed. "What happened?"

Jessica pulled Nick's handkerchief from his suit pocket. Isabella's bluish lips had parted slightly, releasing a trickle of blood. Jessica carefully dabbed the blood, then looked desperately up at the gathered crowd. "Where's that ambulance? Is someone out there to show the medics where we are?"

"They'll be here in two minutes," Alison called out, running up with an armful of blankets. "Where's

Danny?" She looked around. "Someone find Danny Wyatt!"

"He left a while ago," a voice called out.

"Danny's gone?" someone else shouted.

"That guy Clay was the last one with her!" Lila cried. "Has anyone seen him?"

"Who's Clay?" another voice said.

"He's the one we should be tracking down!" Lila sobbed hysterically. "Nick, do something!"

Jessica gave Nick a serious nod of agreement. Then she looked down and carefully spread two blankets over Isabella's still body. Nick whipped out his pocket cell phone and was punching a number.

"Please don't die, Isabella," Jessica murmured, touching Isabella's still, cold forehead. "We'll get you to a hospital. Just . . . hold on. You'll be OK."

"Yeah, Dub. Glad I caught you," Nick murmured into his phone. "Get over here right away. It's the Alpha Chi house on the SVU campus. University Avenue. Four-story house. Big party going on. Woman fell out a window, and paramedics are on their way. But we need a little support here. Yeah. Uh-huh. Right."

"Thank you," Jessica sobbed as she fell into Nick's arms.

Lila stood up and shouted at the crowd forming on the big lawn. "Someone check and see if that guy is still around. Long brown hair."

Tears poured down Jessica's cheeks. "Isn't there anything we could be doing for her now? I mean . . ."

She gently touched Isabella's cold cheek with the palm of her hand. "Isabella?" she whispered. "Can you hear me?"

"Stop touching her, Jess," Nick said gently. "Give us some room, folks," he shouted as the press of curious partygoers drew near. "Medics are on the way. See if you can get those cars out of the driveway for the emergency crews."

Jessica felt a wave of panic as the distant sound of sirens approached. "She's still not moving, Nick," Jessica whimpered. "She's still unconscious."

Nick rubbed his jaw. Then he shook his head and looked up at the balcony, a good three stories above the ground. "It doesn't look good. It doesn't look good at all."

When the ambulance arrived, Nick was relieved to see several Alpha Chis using flashlights to expertly guide the vehicle up the side driveway.

"Stand back, everyone," a uniformed paramedic shouted, rushing to the back of the ambulance.

"Thanks," another medic called out. He slammed his door and ran through the parted crowd.

"She's over here," Nick shouted, waving him over.

Jessica and Lila stood up and took a few steps backward.

"Maybe ten minutes since she fell," Nick told the medic. "She's breathing."

The medic quickly dropped to his knees and bent his ear to Isabella's chest. Then he checked her pulse before placing a pad on the right side of her chest. "I want to get a heart rhythm check here," he shouted to his partner, who was rushing up with more equipment. "Get an IV line going! Stat!"

Nick sucked in his breath. Several patrol cars had pulled behind the ambulance, their sirens whooping at once, then shutting off. The steady whirl of their red lights shone over the scene, and Nick could hear the familiar crackle of the police radio in the background.

"Stand back, miss," a third medic shouted to Jessica. He lowered a gurney to the ground.

Nick grabbed Jessica's shoulders and pulled her close. Her body was trembling, and for the first time he really saw the shock and devastation on her face. "Jess," he whispered.

"We should have caught up with her sooner," she cried softly. "She was running . . . but we didn't know. . . ."

"It's not your fault," Nick murmured. "These guys are going to take care of her—"

"Airways look OK," the first medic shouted. "Looks like we have a break in the right arm. We need something to stabilize that. And get a C collar over here right away."

Nick stood back as the team carefully stabilized Isabella's neck and arm, then lifted her onto the gurney. An IV bag wagged over her motionless body, and a tiny portable screen was bleeping out her unsteady heart rate. A clear oxygen mask had been placed over her nose and mouth.

"We're going to need a trauma surgeon and

neurologist on hand at the ER," one of the medics shouted into a handheld radio.

"Hey, Fox."

Nick loosened his grip on Jessica and turned. Dub Harrison was hurrying toward the scene. He stopped and put one hand on his hip, panting. "How'd you know about this?"

"I was here," Nick explained, rubbing the back of his neck. "Fraternity function. Jessica was invited."

"What's going on?"

"Iz—this woman fell off that balcony," Nick said, nodding toward the balcony. He pulled Dub aside and lowered his voice. "I don't like this. Apparently she was mixed up with some guy no one knew. Happened just before she fell, or—"

Nick and Dub looked at each other and nodded.

"Drugs, maybe?" Dub murmured.

"I'd look into it," Nick replied. He looked over at Jessica, who was huddled with Lila. "Jess? You remember Dub."

"Yeah," Jessica whispered.

"Did you see what happened?" Dub asked.

Jessica shook her head wordlessly and started to cry.

Nick gripped her slender upper arms and pulled her close. "What about Danny Wyatt? Wasn't he her date?"

"Yes."

"So where's he?" Dub asked.

Jessica pressed her lips together. "He left. She— she was talking to Clay DiPalma just before this happened. I told you!"

141

"Danny left about fifteen minutes before this happened," Bruce said, stepping closer and slipping his arm around Lila's waist. "He was upset about something."

"And he just took off?" Nick asked. "Just like that?"

"Isabella and Danny were having problems tonight," Jessica said tearfully. "She'd been telling me about it."

Dub took out a pad and pen. "What was wrong? Was she upset about something in particular? Was she depressed?"

"No!" Jessica protested.

"Are you suggesting that Isabella tried to kill herself?" Lila asked angrily.

Nick turned to Lila. "He just wants to sort out what happened."

The medics slammed the back door of the ambulance, and the siren began to wail.

Jessica brushed away tears. "Isabella was upset because Danny didn't want to come to the party in the first place, and then he wouldn't dance. The next thing I knew, I saw her dancing with Clay DiPalma."

Nick nodded.

Dub wrote down the name. Then he looked up seriously. "Is he here? Did he take off?"

"Yes," Jessica said grimly. "I think he's gone."

"What was she doing with DiPalma?" Nick asked.

Jessica sniffled. "She thought Clay was cute, I guess." She exchanged a serious look with Lila. "After they danced, they were talking together by the front door," Jessica explained. She bit her lower lip. "And then Lila and I noticed that she was starting to act really weird."

Dub stopped writing. "Like how?"

"Well, she was smoking, for one thing," Jessica said.

"A joint?" Dub asked.

"No, it looked like a regular cigarette," Jessica replied. "But Isabella doesn't smoke."

"And then a few minutes later she started acting really freaky," Lila added.

"Sort of drunk," Jessica said.

"But Isabella doesn't drink either," Lila pointed out.

Nick spun around and scanned the crowd. Anger began to rise up inside him like wildfire. "Where is that guy?"

"Hey, Clay didn't follow Isabella upstairs," Jessica insisted. "He didn't have anything to do with this—did he?"

Nick gritted his teeth and began to head quickly across the lawn and around the side of the house, with Jessica, Lila, and Bruce on his tail. "Are you sure she was smoking a cigarette?" he called out over his shoulder.

"Yes," Jessica said impatiently.

"Well, you can lace tobacco with all kinds of drugs," Nick said. He shoved open the house's side door and rushed inside.

Jessica gasped. "You think . . ."

"I can't think," Nick said. "I can't guess. I just need to find out, and Clay's the only person who can tell us if he gave some kind of drug to Isabella."

"You'll never get him to admit that," Jessica said.

"With probable cause, Dub can arrest him and search him," Nick told her. "Those doctors need to know pretty quick what kind of drug is in her body. Sometimes blood work doesn't come back fast enough to help them."

"I bet he won't talk," Lila said, scanning the room. "Eew, I could tell that guy was a lowlife. I'm sure he took off as soon as he figured out what happened."

"Yeah." Nick scoped the nearly empty dance floor. The band was already taking down their equipment. "Anyone see what kind of car he drove?"

Jessica, Lila, and Bruce shook their heads.

"I'm going to check out front," Nick said quickly, ducking through the front door. He shoved his hands in his pockets and walked out onto the front porch and lawn, where a few party-goers were milling about. Everyone was talking quietly as the sound of the ambulance siren faded into the night.

"Drugs," Nick muttered, gritting his teeth. When he first saw Isabella's crumpled body on the ground, he'd suspected it. The scene reminded him of countless other cases he'd investigated in Sweet Valley. Kids too stoned to know they were walking in front of speeding cars. Guys so high, they'd inhaled their own vomit and suffocated. Girls whose hearts had simply given out at the age of seventeen.

Nick circled the building slowly, his eyes scanning the darkness for a face, the ground for a clue.

Nothing.

"Hey, Fox!"

Nick turned and saw Dub hurrying up. "You find anything?"

Nick shook his head. "No. The guy is long gone."

Dub pulled a phone out of his jacket pocket and punched a number. He twirled a toothpick in his mouth as he waited, then took it out. "Chief?" he said. "Yeah. It's Harrison. We've got a serious, possibly drug-related injury over here on the SVU campus. Nineteen-year-old female is on her way to Memorial. We have a description of the kid she was with just before this happened. Put out an APB on this creep—I'd like to have a chat with him. Yeah. Here's Nick. He's got the name and the description."

When Nick was done giving the description, he tracked down Jessica, who was sitting alone on the bottom step of the fraternity's main staircase.

"He took off, didn't he?" Jessica said, leaning into him. She pressed her cheek against Nick's sleeve and began to cry.

Nick felt a catch in his throat. "Yeah."

"I'm sure he knew what happened," Jessica whispered. "He was standing right there when Isabella started freaking. And she ran up the stairs right after that."

Nick took Jessica's hand.

"He *knew*," Jessica wept. "And he just took off."

Nick squeezed her hand. "We'll track him down."

Jessica suddenly turned to him. "And it could have been me."

A horrible, painful lurch rocked Nick's heart.

Jessica was right. It could have been her easily. After all, Clay DiPalma had targeted her first.

Jessica let out a soft, scared cry and clung to his arm even tighter. "If it hadn't been for you . . ."

"Don't think about it," Nick comforted, pulling her close.

"Take me to the hospital," Jessica begged, her face as pale and serious as he'd ever seen it. "I need to be there for Isabella."

"Please let her be OK," Jessica sobbed in Nick's Camaro as they raced toward Sweet Valley Memorial. "I don't care how long it takes. I'm going to sit there until I know she'll be OK."

Nick glanced over at her sympathetically.

Jessica felt a fresh wave of sobs overcome her. Her hair was matted, her eyes were scratchy from crying, she knew her makeup was totally streaked, but she didn't care. All she could think of was Isabella's white, swollen face lying there on the cold earth.

Everything that had seemed so important two days ago had completely evaporated—the big party, the dress she would wear, the sexy pout on Clay DiPalma's mouth, the deep brown eyes that seemed to say so much. . . .

It didn't mean anything, Jessica thought miserably. *It was just a fun game, and now the game is over.*

Nick sped through the parking lot entrance and quickly found a spot. Jessica was out the passenger-side door practically before he'd stopped.

"Wait up, Jess," he called.

Jessica took off her heels and panted. For a moment all she could do was stand there in a confused panic.

"It doesn't look good for Izzy, does it?" Jessica whispered as Nick caught up with her and slipped his arm around her waist.

Nick rubbed his eyes. "It could go either way, Jess. I've seen suicides drop three stories down and walk away."

Jessica stared straight ahead as they walked. She felt angry heat rising in her cheeks.

"It depends on how they fall," Nick explained, leading her through Sweet Valley Memorial's automatic doors. "Or maybe it's just fate."

She was hit by the aroma of antiseptic. How she hated that smell. She made a fist. "She *has* to be OK."

"It might depend on what was in her system."

"Do you really think Clay slipped her some kind of drug?" Jessica asked.

Their eyes met and locked. "Oh yeah," Nick said firmly.

"But what kind? Something you can put into a cigarette?"

Nick pointed toward the emergency-room sign. "You can put lots of chemicals into tobacco."

Jessica felt sick. "Like what?"

"Marijuana, heroin, cocaine," Nick went on. He raked his hair back with his fingers and pushed open the emergency-room entrance for Jessica. "PCP."

Jessica nodded. "Angel dust."

"Yeah," Nick said. "It gives the user an insane high. I've seen it before."

Jessica bit back tears. A nurse hurried by, checking her watch. Up ahead, she could see the crowded waiting room. An icy cold feeling went up her spine. "How could someone sneak that to someone? You'd have to be totally depraved."

Nick sighed and shook his head as they approached the reception area. "Maybe he thought she'd like it," he said bitterly. "Maybe he thought he could capture another paying customer. I mean—if that's what actually happened."

"Isabella didn't look like she was enjoying herself," Jessica said sadly.

"No. I've seen a few people get really paranoid on that drug," Nick said, tapping his fingers on the waiting-room counter. "They get claustrophobic. They think they're being chased or attacked."

"Maybe that's what happened to Izzy," Jessica thought out loud. "She was acting so weird—like— like she couldn't stand to have anyone near her. Like she had to get away."

Nick cursed under his breath.

"May I help you?" a nurse asked hurriedly.

"Isabella Ricci?" Jessica asked quickly. "They just brought her in here for . . ."

"Yes," the nurse said crisply. "The doctors are examining her right now in the ER." She pointed toward a bank of sagging couches. "Please have a seat, and we'll let you know what's going on when we can."

Jessica and Nick slowly walked over and sat down. Across from them a tired, unshaven man sat with a little boy. In the corner to their left a heavy, gray-haired woman sat alone holding her purse and blowing her nose.

"I just wish . . . ," Nick finally said.

Jessica turned. "Wish what?"

Nick leaned forward and held his head in his hands. "I just had a bad feeling about that guy. I should have—"

"What could you have done?" Jessica protested. "You already punched him out because he was coming on to *me*."

"Yeah, but—"

"He must have seen you there at the party," Jessica reasoned. "And that didn't seem to discourage him."

Nick made a fist. "I could have shared a few choice words with him. Warned him. Maybe taken him aside, just so he knew he was still being watched . . ."

"It's not your fault," Jessica said, taking his arm and pulling him close. The strain of the night showed clearly in his eyes under the bright fluorescent lights.

She felt a swell of bittersweet emotion. It was funny how things worked out sometimes. When she fell in love with Nick, she thought it was partly because he'd swept her up in the kind of real-life excitement she'd longed for all her life.

Now she was beginning to see the real truth. Nick wasn't about danger. He was about being safe and honest and strong. And that's what she needed more than anything: a steadying force in her crazy, up-and-down life.

Jessica bit her lip. Why did she have to wait for a terrible crisis to figure this out—to make her realize what was really important in her life?

Nick gazed at her tenderly. "Thanks, Jess."

Jessica looked back into his green eyes. "Tell me something."

"What?" he said, snuggling closer on the vinyl seat.

"How did you know?"

Nick turned toward her a little and cradled her chin in his hand. "Know what, Jess?"

"How did you know that Clay DiPalma was trouble?" Jessica asked shyly.

Nick shrugged. "I just knew."

Jessica looked seriously into his eyes. "But how? Was it a hunch?"

Nick shifted around in his seat and put his hands on Jessica's shoulders. "I got used to looking for a certain type."

Jessica bit her lip. How could she have been so stupid? It was Clay's *look* that had attracted her to him in the first place. Only a few days ago, in fact, she'd actually considered dumping Nick because of it. What was it? His face? The way he moved his body? The way he looked at her? How could she have even *thought* of risking so much based on so little?

"And I've seen that type before," Nick went on. "He had that slick, I'm-so-tough look. It was the cocky way he walked. A kind of overconfidence. You see that, and you think, Hey, he's got something to hide behind all that body language."

Jessica brushed away the tears on her cheeks. "I've got to tell you something."

"What's that?" Nick asked, stroking her hair and smiling.

Jessica looked directly into his eyes. "I'm never going to doubt you again."

Chapter
Ten

"What room did Jessica say Isabella was in?" Danny asked, rushing off the elevator.

"She's in the ICU," Tom reminded him. "Don't you remember? It's down that way."

Danny clasped his hand to his forehead. "If anything happens to her . . ."

"Steady," Tom warned. "Come on. Let's see what the doctors say first."

Danny looked down the wide hospital corridor. An orderly walked by, pushing a stainless steel cart. A nurse yanked open a supply cabinet and pulled out a plastic-wrapped package. To the right several doctors bustled about a nurses' station. He and Tom hurried toward it.

"Isabella Ricci?" Danny asked. His throat closed up with fear.

The nurse typing on the other side of the counter slipped on her glasses. She reached over and picked up a clipboard. "She's critical but stable and out of

ICU." She pointed down the hall. "Go through those double doors. Room four twenty-eight."

Danny rushed through the double doors into the hallway, then slowed when he neared Isabella's room.

"I guess we can just go in," Tom assured him. He glanced at the room number, then turned the doorknob and pushed the door open for Danny.

Without looking up, he walked into the room. He stood still for a moment, unable to actually acknowledge the person in the bed.

"Looks like she's still really out of it," Tom whispered.

Danny finally turned his head and let his eyes lock onto the frail, motionless body. Isabella's body. A body that seemed barely there under the rumple of white sheets and blankets. A bank of machines and bleeping monitors stood over the head of the bed.

"Man, they're really . . . uh . . . pulling out all the stops for her, huh?" Tom said quietly.

Finally Danny let his eyes travel up to her face, where they lingered in stony disbelief. It was Isabella, all right. But barely. Plastic tubes were clamped against her cheeks. An IV line had been punched into her left arm. Her neck was encased in a neck brace, and her right arm was in a cast.

"Isabella," he whispered. He told himself to stay in control, but he couldn't help but feel anger and confusion welling up inside him like a volcano.

Danny took a step forward, gazing in shock at her chalk white cheeks. A large white bandage covered her forehead, and her right cheekbone was so bruised and swollen, one eye had almost completely disappeared from view.

"Isabella?" Danny repeated. "Can you hear me?"

Isabella's one visible eye remained closed. Her face was completely still.

"Izzy?"

Danny felt Tom's hand on his shoulder. A sudden, painful wave washed over him. He had to press his lips tightly together to hold it in.

"She's still unconscious, Danno."

Danny's heart sickened. Gently he slipped his hand into Isabella's and studied her long, slender fingers.

"What did the nurses say?" Tom asked. "That she was stable?"

Danny's anger rose up. "She doesn't look stable to me. She looks like she's slipping away." He looked back at the door and shouted, *We need a doctor in here!*

"Hey, hey, hey," Tom urged him. "Cool it. They're doing their best—"

"It's not good enough!" Danny interrupted loudly, making a fist. "Look at her. She jumped off a balcony. What made her want to do that?"

"Good morning," he heard a brisk voice behind him. Danny turned around and saw a tall woman with salt-and-pepper hair in a white jacket stride into the room. "I'm Dr. Gomez," she said. "Are you friends of Ms. Ricci's?"

"Yes," Danny croaked. "I'm Danny Wyatt. This is my friend Tom Watts."

Dr. Gomez checked several monitors, then felt Isabella's wrist for a pulse. She lifted Isabella's eyelids and pointed a small flashlight into Isabella's pupils—lifeless, blank, and unseeing. Danny winced and looked away.

"SVU students?" the doctor asked pleasantly.

"Yes," Danny said quickly. "Look. I—we really need to know what's going on. We're not family or anything, but . . ."

"Her family has been contacted and will be here in a few hours," Dr. Gomez explained. "Mr. and Mrs. Ricci authorized me to release information to you, Mr. Wyatt. They were quite sure you'd be here."

Danny felt his panic rise.

The doctor's expression turned grave. "Isabella is in critical condition. Aside from her broken arm and deep lacerations and bruising on her face and back and left side, she has a subdural hematoma—a potentially serious head injury."

"What?" Danny cried.

"It's a small bleed inside her skull that resulted from the trauma of the fall," Dr. Gomez said. "The trouble with these bleeds is that they can result in coma and serious brain damage if they don't stabilize. And sometimes that doesn't happen for a while. Which is why we have to watch her carefully."

"But can't you do something now?" Tom asked. "Surgery or . . ."

Dr. Gomez looked down at her clipboard and shook her head. "The trauma surgeons and neurologists who have examined her want to wait. We want to see if she regains consciousness first. Then we'll need to run regular tests on her neurological functions because—"

"Because what?" Danny whispered.

"Because even if she does regain consciousness, she may still go downhill," Dr. Gomez said soberly.

Danny groaned and shaded his eyes with one hand.

"Do you know for sure what caused this?" Tom asked. "Some of our friends thought she was slipped some kind of drug."

Dr. Gomez leaned against the edge of the bed and crossed her arms. "I just received the final lab report a few minutes ago. We found traces of PCP in her blood." Dr. Gomez gave them a cool look. "Can you explain that?"

"Oh no," Danny groaned. Tom tried to pat his shoulder, but Danny flinched and moved away.

"Angel dust," Tom said in disbelief.

"Yes," Dr. Gomez confirmed.

Danny looked at Tom in shock. "I can't believe she'd do that."

"Come on, man," Tom protested. "Don't you see? Someone probably slipped it to her."

Danny's eyes blazed back at him. "Who? She wouldn't hang around with someone like that!"

"It's a synthetic drug," Dr. Gomez explained. "It originally was a veterinary tranquilizer. . . ."

Danny's heart pounded agonizingly. "Tranquilizer . . . what . . . I don't want to know. I mean, this is just too—"

"Chill," Tom urged.

"The drug produces a kind of hallucinogenic high that's popular with some drug users," Dr. Gomez continued. "Very small amounts can produce big reactions that last for hours."

"Could someone have slipped it to her?" Tom asked.

Dr. Gomez nodded. "She might not have known at all. Angel dust can be incorporated into an ordinary cigarette. . . ."

"*What?*" Danny exclaimed. He looked at Isabella's motionless body with fresh shock. "She *was* smoking. She was smoking with that lowlife she picked up at Alpha Chi."

"Maybe that was it," Tom said softly.

"It wasn't as if she was completely taken advantage of," Danny cried out. "She didn't *have* to take that cigarette. No one *forced* her to hang with a guy who looked like he just got his drug-dealing degree."

"Come on, man," Tom pleaded. "Let the doctor speak."

"The trouble with PCP," Dr. Gomez went on, "is that it often brings on severe delusions, visual disturbances, and anxiety. I've seen kids who thought they were being attacked by animals or insects. And I've seen others, like Isabella, feel so certain they needed to escape, they've also jumped out windows—even through glass. Kids on this drug don't even feel any pain."

"But I wasn't even there," Danny suddenly burst out. He stood up abruptly and walked over to the window. The Sunday morning sunshine seemed unforgivingly bright. "I *left* the party like an idiot. I don't *know* if she jumped. Maybe someone pushed her!"

"Danny," Tom warned. He gripped Danny's shoulder. "Jessica didn't think so."

"Isabella was acting so crazy," Danny went on, "even before she hooked up with him . . . dancing with ten guys at once. I told her to stop. That she was making a fool of herself. I told her to leave with me—that I w-wanted to protect her," he stammered. He took a breath. "But she wouldn't listen. . . ."

"It's going to be OK," Tom murmured.

Danny shoved him away. "No, it's not. She wouldn't let me protect her. And now she's . . . she's . . . How could she do this to herself? How could she do this to *me?*"

But before he could choke out the rest of his angry thoughts, Danny ducked down his head, pushed past Dr. Gomez, and ran out of Isabella's hospital room.

Jessica grabbed her sweater, purse, and keys. "Come on, Elizabeth. It's already eight A.M. We can be at the hospital in fifteen minutes if we hurry."

"OK," Elizabeth said, unhooking her dorm key from the wall and pulling on a sweatshirt. "Let's go."

They quickly slipped out of the dead-quiet dorm and ran across the parking lot to their Jeep.

"I'll drive," Jessica said hurriedly.

"Take Pacific Avenue," Elizabeth said, slamming

the passenger door shut. "It's much faster."

"Please let her be OK. Please let her be OK," Jessica chanted in a soft voice as she tore out of the parking lot and onto the main drag off campus.

She felt Elizabeth's hand on her shoulder. "It's not your fault, Jess."

Jessica tried to shake off tears and focus on the road. The night before, she and Nick had been turned away by the nurses staff. All they'd been able to do was tell doctors how to reach Isabella's parents.

At four o'clock in the morning Jessica had called the hospital to check on Isabella, only to get a cryptic message about how she was still in critical condition.

"You didn't sleep at all last night, did you?" Elizabeth asked gently.

Jessica shook her head. All night she'd tossed and turned, her mind spinning with memories of the night before.

"I feel so guilty about this," Jessica admitted tearfully.

"Jess, remember, it's not your fault," Elizabeth soothed.

"But maybe if I hadn't—"

"Hadn't *what?*"

Jessica wiped away a tear. "Isabella came up to me during the party and told me she'd noticed Clay. And all I could do was sort of nod and wink and let her know how cute *I* thought he was too."

"Oh, Jess—"

"What I should have told her was *stay away!*"

Jessica said. "I should have told her that Nick had really bad feelings about him."

"But you said Nick warned her," Elizabeth reasoned.

"Yes," Jessica said tearfully. "He warned us both. But don't you understand? She was feeling really rebellious. She wasn't going to listen to some *guy* tell her what to do. But she might have listened to *me*."

"You're being too hard on yourself."

Jessica tapped the steering wheel nervously. "All I could do was say *'oooh, isn't he great?'* when all along I should have known he was trouble."

Elizabeth reached over and stroked her sister's shoulder.

Jessica felt hot tears. "Clay DiPalma. He's perfect. He's just the kind of guy who always shows up when your love life is on the rocks. It happened to me. And then it happened to Isabella. Only she wasn't so lucky."

Jessica shook her head in frustration. She drove quickly past Sweet Valley's downtown shopping area, the bus station, the library, and the pleasant west-side neighborhoods until they reached the hospital, nestled among palm trees on the side of a hill.

"Please be OK," Jessica kept muttering to herself as she and her sister hurried through the hospital's main lobby. She almost ran straight into Danny. He was standing all by himself, his hands on his hips and his head low and shaking, as if he were terribly upset.

"Danny?" Jessica cried out. "How is she? Is she OK?"

Danny looked up, and Jessica could see the muscles in his jaw tightening. His red-rimmed eyes blazed.

"Danny?" Jessica repeated, scared. "What's . . ."

"I can't talk," Danny said quickly. "She's in room four twenty-eight."

"What?" Elizabeth said.

"Four twenty-eight," he blurted. Then he turned. And before Jessica or Elizabeth could say another word, he was rushing away down the hall.

"Do you think something's happened?" Jessica grabbed Elizabeth's arm.

"I don't know," Elizabeth said quietly.

Jessica shuddered. After checking in at the reception area, the two made their way down the silent hallway and slowly pushed open the door to Isabella's room. At first, all Jessica could see was a sober-looking Tom standing next to a doctor in a white jacket. Then she saw Isabella, asleep on the bed behind them, her body attached to a web of tubing and IVs. A heart monitor bleeped above her head.

Jessica drew her hands up to her mouth to keep from sobbing out loud. Isabella's slender neck was in a cushioned brace, and her right arm was in a cast. But worst of all was Isabella's face—gray-white, swollen, and absolutely still.

"We just saw Danny . . . ," Elizabeth said.

"He's pretty upset," Tom said, taking Elizabeth's hand. He nodded toward the doctor. "Dr.

161

Gomez. This is Elizabeth and Jessica Wakefield. They're close friends of Isabella's. Jessica was with her at the party."

Jessica sucked in her breath as the doctor stepped forward. Dr. Gomez's face was terribly, horribly serious. She settled a clipboard onto her hip and glanced up at the monitor. Then she gave the three of them a sober look. "We've found traces of the drug PCP in Isabella's bloodstream. Do any of you know about this?"

Jessica gasped. "Isabella's never been interested in drugs," she said. "She doesn't even drink very much. I mean, Danny would freak. He freaks if Isabella doesn't get enough *wheat germ* in her diet."

Tom nodded toward the hall. "He just found out. That's why he took off. He's pretty upset about it."

Jessica looked up at the doctor. "Is she going to be OK?"

"She has a severe brain bleed called a subdural hematoma," Dr. Gomez told her. "We're going to have to wait and see."

"The doctor says there's a chance Isabella could slip into a coma," Tom said softly.

Jessica threw her arms around her sister and sobbed.

"Is there anything we can do?" Elizabeth asked the doctor. "Would it help to sit with her? Talk to her?"

Dr. Gomez placed her hand on Elizabeth's shoulder. "I think that would be fine. She'll need all the support she can get."

"Anything we can do. *Anything.*" Jessica wrung her hands and gazed down at Isabella's broken body. She shuddered with fear. On top of everything else, she couldn't help realizing that if it hadn't been for Nick, *she* would have been Clay's victim. *She* would have been lying in a hospital bed with a broken body—or worse.

Nick Fox. If he was a protector, then so be it. Maybe part of being strong and independent was having the ability to accept protection from others. Maybe it was time for Jessica to stop fighting so much.

"Isabella . . . oh, my little girl."

Jessica looked up. A small, dark-haired woman in a long dark dress had entered the room and was bent carefully over Isabella, tenderly cradling the side of her face. "We got here just as soon as we heard, my darling daughter," the woman said in a soft, tearful voice.

Behind the woman was an older, balding man dressed in a polo shirt and khakis. Jessica watched sadly as the man slumped onto the edge of Isabella's bed and shook his head. His eyes, which looked exactly like Isabella's, stared hopelessly into space. "My little girl," he whispered.

"Maybe it's time to go," Elizabeth whispered as Dr. Gomez approached Isabella's parents.

Jessica nodded. Together with Tom and Elizabeth, she slipped out quietly. But Jessica's thoughts were anything but quiet. She knew with every fiber of her being that she and Nick had to nail Clay DiPalma to the wall.

For Isabella, it was the least they could do.

*   *   *

"I've got to cut this down to forty-five seconds," Tom mumbled. He poised his red pen over a WSVU transcript and frowned.

Outside Reid Hall, the sun was shining. Tom could hear the shouts from the dorm's Sunday afternoon pickup flag football game on the field below. A dog barked. Down the hallway, he could hear the ding of the elevator and muffled laughter.

He glanced over and saw that Danny was still sitting at his desk, hunched over a textbook. His back was just as stiff and perfectly straight as it was the last time he looked. In fact, Danny had barely moved at all in the last hour.

"Catch some football?" Tom asked, checking his watch. "They've just started out there."

"Nope."

Tom shook his head sadly. Since they got back from the hospital that morning, Danny hadn't spoken one word. All he could manage to do was shuffle dryly through his microbiology textbook and stare at the bulletin board in front of him.

"Look, Danny—"

"Put a lid on it, Tom," Danny said. "I'm sorry, man, but I just can't—"

"Yeah. OK," Tom said quickly, holding his hands up in defeat. He knew he shouldn't even try to make Danny feel better, but he couldn't help it. Another scenario kept repeating in his mind: What if it had been him and Elizabeth who had fought? What if he had left her in a fit of anger? And what if it had been *Elizabeth* who'd accidentally taken a drug that had given her the crazy idea to jump off a balcony?

Tom squeezed his eyes closed, trying to imagine the agony. The guilt. The fear that she'd never get up out of that hospital bed.

Tom slipped the transcript off his lap and placed it on the bed. He grabbed a Nerf basketball off his desk and batted it between his hands. "Shoot a few baskets?" he asked, unable to help himself.

"Forget it."

Tom took aim at the mini–basketball net clamped to the top of his closet door. He tossed, missed, and scooped it up again with his outstretched arm.

"You've got to eat. Let's go grab a pizza. It's on me."

"I'm going to study for a while."

"Look, Danny," Tom said. "It's not your fault, you know."

"Shut up, Watts."

Tom stopped shooting baskets and sighed. "That's what you think, don't you? You think it's your fault Isabella Ricci is lying in the hospital right now."

Danny slowly looked up from his textbook and turned his face toward Tom, his eyes blazing with fury. "I said shut up."

"And let me tell you something else, Wyatt," Tom went on firmly, "it's not Isabella's fault either. She didn't know what that creep was giving her when she—"

Danny slammed his book shut and stared at the cover. "She knew *exactly* what she was doing."

Tom let out a shocked half laugh. "You're kidding . . . right?"

Danny turned to face him again. Beads of sweat had broken out on his forehead. His jaw had stiffened, and his eyebrows were drawn together so tightly that deep furrows had formed on his forehead. "Would you like to know what Isabella said to me just before I left the Alpha Chi party?"

"Come on, Danno. Don't do this."

"She said, 'You just watch and see how much fun I can have tonight. I will never regret it.' *That's* what she said to me."

"But . . . she was angry with you, man," Tom tried to explain.

"You're right about that, Tom."

"We all get ticked off sometimes," Tom struggled. "I mean, it sounds like she . . . she just lost her temper."

"Uh-huh."

Tom bit his lip and tried to find something else to say. "I don't think she meant it. That's all I'm trying to tell you."

Danny shook his head angrily. "She meant it."

Tom slammed the basketball down onto the floor. "Hold on. She *meant* to jump out of a window and nearly kill herself? Is that what you're trying to say?"

For a moment Danny just sat there. Then he suddenly stood up, knocking over his desk chair. "She *deserved* what she got!"

"*What?*"

"She was looking for trouble," Danny cried. "She deliberately ignored my advice and protection. Yeah. She deserved what she got."

"Y-You can't mean that, Danny."

"I mean it, Watts." Without another word Danny bolted out the door and slammed it behind him.

"Who's in today, Betty?" Nick asked the Sweet Valley precinct's receptionist.

Betty smiled. "I thought you were on leave, Detective. You sure don't look like it."

"Sometimes I think I've got this job in my blood."

"Oh yeah?" Betty asked good-naturedly. "Well, maybe you should just come on back."

Nick leaned over the counter. "Something happened last night at one of the SVU fraternities that made me think about it."

The receptionist nodded as the phone rang. "And you need some answers, huh? Chief Wallace and Dub are off today, but Artie Snyder's in." She looked over her shoulder. "There he is. In the back room at the computer. He's doing some background research, I think."

"Thanks," Nick said quickly, slipping past the counter and through the back door into a cluttered area crammed with computers and floor-to-ceiling files.

Hunched over a keyboard was his old friend Detective Artie Snyder, a veteran of the Sweet

Valley police force, known for his string of successful white-collar crime busts over the past decade. If anyone in the precinct could point him in the right direction, Snyder was definitely the man.

"Hey, Nick," Artie said, looking up and pushing back his chair. He had a wide waistline and gray, grizzled eyebrows that shaded his piercing blue eyes. "How's my favorite college boy?"

Nick laughed and leaned against a table, where a fax machine was spitting out a long series of pages. "Good, good."

"Still going out with the beautiful Miss Jessica?" Artie asked.

"I sure am."

"Been to any wild college parties lately?"

Nick winked. "I'm always hitting the wild parties, Artie. That's what I need to talk to you about."

"What can I help you with?"

Nick rubbed his jawline thoughtfully. "I'm trying to track someone down."

Artie shrugged. "What for? You don't have to get into this stuff anymore. You're a free man."

"Yeah, I know," Nick tried to explain. "It's just—it's just something I've got to figure out. Call it a case of simple curiosity."

Artie leaned back in his chair and twiddled his thumbs on his ample stomach. "OK. Look. I can check it out for you, but do me a favor and don't go haywire with it, OK? It's against precinct policy. We don't do research for curious civilians who come strolling in on Sunday afternoons."

168

Nick smiled.

"Now what's this about?"

"A guy calling himself Clay DiPalma showed up at a fraternity function last night and passed on a PCP-laced cigarette to a young woman there. Harrison was there. He's on it."

Artie whistled. "Just can't stay away, can you?"

"She's Jessica's friend," Nick explained. "And she had a pretty bad reaction to the stuff. In fact, she walked right off a balcony a few minutes later. Now she's lying in the hospital, and I'm not sure if she's ever going to get up."

Snyder narrowed his eyes. "What's he look like?"

"Six feet, shoulder-length medium-brown hair, brown eyes, fairly slight build, cocky stride," Nick said. "Probably about twenty, twenty-one years old."

Artie stuffed his hands in his pockets. "Lot of drugs coming through Sweet Valley right now. Bad stuff. We're seeing heroin in the suburban areas. And PCP is real popular right now on campus."

"That's what I'm after," Nick said.

Artie punched several keys on his computer and sat back. "We've been following a creep named Nelson Karl for the past couple of months." A photograph and description suddenly flicked onto the screen. "He's originally from the Miami area, but he's made L.A. his base for now."

"Whew." Nick chuckled. "That guy has one ugly mug."

Artie laughed too. "Yeah. They call him 'The Nose,' actually, thanks to his notorious fondness for cocaine *and* the bulbous proportions of his nasal anatomy."

Nick shook his head. "Nelson 'The Nose' Karl, huh?"

"Yep," Artie said, typing into the computer. "We've had our folks input into the database descriptions of all Nelson Karl's known associates. If you like, we can try to cross-link your description of this Clay DiPalma."

"Go for it," Nick said eagerly. He felt his blood pumping the way it used to when he was on the force. But this time it was different. Clay DiPalma wasn't just a guy who nearly killed Isabella Ricci. He was a guy who'd seriously messed with Jessica. And as long as a guy like that was hanging around the SVU campus, Nick could never be sure Jessica was safe.

Artie punched in Nick's description. "DiPalma's probably a cover, of course."

Nick nodded. "Don't doubt it."

"Kid hurt pretty bad, huh?"

"Yeah," Nick said. "Bad head injury, I guess. Never know how those cases turn out."

Artie grunted in disgust. But then his eyes brightened when something popped up on the screen.

"Hey," Nick said, leaning over Artie's shoulder. "Look at that."

Artie scratched the back of his neck. "Mmmm. I don't know, Nick. This *could* be what you're looking for." He tapped his pencil on the screen. "Your description somewhat matches a guy called Corey Parsons."

Nick moved closer to the screen and studied it. "Corey Parsons. Arrested on drug-trafficking charges in September of last year. No conviction. Looks like he got off on a technicality there, Artie."

"Yep. I know this guy," Artie said thoughtfully. "Seen him with The Nose several times. You're right. He's kind of a cocky guy. Young stud sort of fellow. Likes the ladies. And they like him."

"Yeah," Nick said, pacing.

Artie let out a nervous chuckle. "Uh. Look, Nick, buddy. There really isn't enough here to know for sure if this Parsons is your guy. We don't have an alias listed for him. No photo. Just a description."

Nick nodded seriously. "I hear you."

Artie gave him a warning look. "You're not going to go and string this guy up yourself now, right?"

Nick smiled at him. "Artie."

Artie held his hands up in defense. "I had to ask. You could land in deep water if you go out there acting like a Big Cop on Campus without backup."

"Don't worry about it," Nick assured him, slapping Artie's shoulder and turning to leave. "And thanks a lot, pal."

Chapter Eleven

"That should do it," Elizabeth said firmly as she typed out the last few words of her article at the *Gazette* on Monday morning.

She sat back in her chair and took a gulp of stale coffee. It was a long story and sidebar on Isabella's accident—not an easy story to do, but one she'd eagerly volunteered for. Isabella deserved to have her story told by someone who could write it well.

"OK." She slowly set the cardboard cup down next to her keyboard. Then she checked her research notes, stared into space for a moment, and bent back down to her work.

"Give it a break, Elizabeth," Ed Greyson said. He gave her a tired smile. "You've been at it for two hours."

Elizabeth rubbed her eyes. "I really want to write a good story on this. For Isabella's sake."

Ed leaned against Elizabeth's desk and looked at her clipboard. "You're our lead story."

"I'll zap it over to you in about five minutes. The main story is about a thousand words. And the sidebar on PCP is about five hundred."

"Check," Ed said. "Two hours ahead of deadline too. Good work."

Elizabeth checked her watch. "Thanks."

"Still pretty upset about Isabella, aren't you?"

Elizabeth nodded. "Especially after writing up all the gruesome details. I just wish I could have seen it coming. But I wasn't even at that party. It was a Greek thing."

"And she's still not conscious, is she?"

"No. They're watching her really carefully for bleeding in the brain." Elizabeth trembled as she grabbed a hair clip out of her top drawer and twisted her long blond hair into a messy bun. "Her parents are there now."

"They haven't found the sleaze who did this to her?"

Elizabeth shook her head and wiped a stray tear. "You know what I can't get over? I just can't get over the fact that a lowlife drug dealer like that could stroll right into a private fraternity party and start slipping drugs to unsuspecting students."

Ed shrugged. "Yeah. But what can you do? Station bodyguards with metal detectors around the punch bowl?"

"I don't know what the answer is." She pointed to her screen. "Except maybe this."

Ed nodded.

Elizabeth flipped through a stack of notes and pulled out a piece of paper. "I guess we have to keep our eyes open every second now, even when we're out just having a good time."

"Drag," Ed agreed, giving Elizabeth a weak salute and heading toward his office. "Thanks again for the good work."

"Yeah," Elizabeth said, staring wearily at her full screen, then suddenly spotting her blinking e-mail message light. She clicked out of her document and called up her messages, the last one from an Edie Monroe.

Elizabeth tapped her pencil on the edge of her desk and clicked the name with her mouse. Where had she seen that name before?

A moment later a short message, followed by a long article, appeared on her screen.

Elizabeth,
   I know that you used to work with Scott, so I knew you'd want to know about this right away. Please e-mail or phone back if you need to talk.
                        Edie

Elizabeth's eyes opened wide as she began to read the long article that followed, under a headline that read:

DCIR EXPELS STAR INVESTIGATIVE REPORTER
BY EDIE MONROE

"What?" Elizabeth cried softly, scrolling down and staring in amazement at what followed.

DCIR undergrad Scott Sinclair was expelled by university authorities yesterday after an exclusive *Tribune* investigation revealed a disturbing pattern of falsified documents and manufactured interviews in articles he wrote for this publication.

Elizabeth gasped as she continued to read.

Nineteen-year-old Sinclair was a recent transfer from Sweet Valley University in California, where he was a reporter for its award-winning student daily newspaper, the *Gazette*.

Sinclair now has admitted to university officials that he faked much of the information in a series of recent *Tribune* articles concerning a credit card fraud involving hundreds of Colorado college students.

Sinclair was unavailable for comment today, and sources close to the student have told the *Tribune* that he has left for his family home in Montana.

On Monday, Dean of Admissions Thomas A. Lacey also revealed that Sinclair had illegally altered his transcripts from Sweet Valley University, boosting his grade point average as well as falsifying many of the awards he had claimed on his application.

In addition, the university was bombarded with many complaints from Mr. Sinclair's coworkers at the *Tribune*, claiming that the reporter took credit for much of the research conducted by colleagues. . . .

"Edie Monroe," Elizabeth gasped. She had been the reporter who had shared Scott's byline on the article he'd e-mailed to her about the fraud. Edie Monroe had probably had enough of Scott taking credit for her work.

Elizabeth buried her face in her hands. Scott Sinclair. It was true that he'd been aggressive, curious, smart, and a good interviewer. But it was also true that she herself had done him the favor of writing up articles from his notes more than once.

And he always had such great excuses, Elizabeth thought with disgust. And always Elizabeth had saved him. *She* had written the articles and done the important background research that gave them credibility. *She* had single-handedly turned his dry, scribbled notes into the sharp and moving articles that had won them praise and recognition.

It was all becoming very clear. Scott Sinclair had probably wooed plenty of smart young women reporters for the same purpose. Now she knew why Scott had wanted her to come with him to Denver so badly. He never could have made it there on his own.

Elizabeth shuddered. How could she have fallen for his flattery? How could she have let him pull her in like that? A romance? He never loved her.

She had come so close to leaving SVU and joining Scott in Denver. If she hadn't followed her heart, she would have been stuck out there with no one—discredited and alone.

A small smile began to spread across her face as she felt the load of uncertainty lift away from her heart. She *had* made the right decision. She had missed nothing. She could now write Scott Sinclair out of her life forever.

Elizabeth double-clicked the reply icon. *Dear Edie,* Elizabeth typed, her hands shaking with emotion. *Thank you so much for writing. You've answered a lot of my questions.* . . .

"We'll take a look at the growth curve for an exponentially increasing bacterial population, plotted logarithmically and arithmetically," Professor Jacobson droned on. "I especially want your study emphasis to be on the four basic phases of growth."

Danny squinted at the overhead projection and copied Professor Jacobson's final notations. Then his gaze slipped away for a moment toward the large paned window to his right.

It was eleven o'clock, and his Monday morning biology class was about to be dismissed. He checked his watch and flashed back to Sunday morning, when he was in Isabella's hospital room, staring in shock at her broken body and wondering how things could have gone so terribly wrong. He squeezed his eyes shut. He didn't want to think about it. Where was his concentration?

Face it. Isabella is impulsive, attention seeking, and flighty. I fell in love with her, but I don't know if I should have. She won't let me be there for her. And how can I, when I never know what to expect?

Danny leaned back in his chair and drew a tower of small, precise arrows in the margin of his notes. It was strange. When he first dated Isabella, he'd actually been attracted to her spontaneous, passionate nature. Back then, he used words like *fun loving* and *enthusiastic* to describe her. It had been exciting to break the study-grind mold at first.

And then there was Isabella's beautiful, perfect face looking up at him like an open flower. Her long black hair that slipped back over her shoulders like silk. Who could have resisted her?

Danny twirled his pen, then drew it up to his lips and bit down hard on the cap. He knew he should be kneeling at Isabella's bedside right now, asking for forgiveness and begging her to get well. But he couldn't let go of the anger.

Isabella was *responsible* for what happened to her. She waltzed off with an obvious scumbag and took a puff of the first thing he pulled out of his grubby, lowlife pocket. What did she expect? His approval? His forgiveness?

Danny pressed his pen into his notebook page until it snapped out of his hand and pinged onto the floor.

"Mr. Wyatt?" Professor Jacobson said loudly, interrupting Danny's thoughts. "Are we disturbing you?"

Danny looked up and cleared his throat. The class had turned to look at him, and a hush had fallen over the room. "Uh. No. I'm sorry, did you ask me a question?"

Professor Jacobson placed her two gnarled hands on the lab counter and smiled. "Yes, I did ask you a question, Mr. Wyatt."

Danny straightened. "Oh. OK. Well—"

"My question was," Professor Jacobson went on, "what is the most frequently used method for the measurement of bacterial populations?"

Danny coughed, looked down, and began flipping nervously through his textbook. "Um. I'm not sure . . . but—"

"Thank you, Mr. Wyatt," the professor cut him off. "That's all I needed to know." She closed her book and looked severely at the class. "You will be examined on all of this material on Friday. And I guarantee it will be no picnic. It will be a full, one-hour exam with only a limited number of multiple-choice questions. Most will require short answers and essays. So be prepared, and I will see you on Wednesday for our final review."

Danny stood and gathered his things.

"Mr. Wyatt," he heard his professor call out as he headed out the side door. "May I see you for a moment?"

"Yes?" Danny said, approaching.

Professor Jacobson's wrinkled face looked even more pinched than usual. "I'm worried about you."

Danny rubbed the back of his neck and looked down. "You are?"

"Of course I am," she snapped.

Danny stiffened.

Her eyes bored into him. "You showed a great deal of promise at the beginning of the semester, and I don't enjoy watching you destroy your grade."

"Destroy my grade?"

Danny set his books and notebook down on Professor Jacobson's cluttered lab desk. "Things aren't that bad, are they?"

Professor Jacobson grabbed a spiral notebook and flipped through it. "I'm seeing grades in your lab work and class quizzes drop from the high ninetieth percentile to the low eighties."

"Oh yes."

"This is unacceptable for someone with your obvious talent and drive," Professor Jacobson told him. "You're headed for graduate school, young man. And you can't afford to blow your grade in my class."

"Yes, well, I've had some personal distractions . . . ," he stammered before he stopped himself in shame. Was he actually going to complain about Isabella's nonsense in front of this eminent microbiologist?

"Control your distractions," she demanded. "Rise above them." She leaned down and scribbled something on a piece of paper. "Do this supplemental reading before Friday. It will help you prepare."

"Thank you," Danny said softly, taking her note.

"I expect miracles from you, Wyatt," she snapped, turning away and packing her briefcase.

Danny quickly grabbed his books and hurried

out of the classroom, his face hot with anger and shame. It was bad enough that his troubles with Isabella were distracting him from his studies. But totally rock-bottom that even his *professors* were starting to notice.

"What do you think Clay DiPalma is doing right this minute?" Jessica said between gritted teeth.

Nick looked up from the thick university catalog on his lap. Then he checked his watch. "Seven o'clock Monday night. He should be slithering back down into his snake pit right now."

Jessica readjusted her pillow on Nick's couch and draped her legs over his. "Actually, I'm serious."

Nick looked down. "I'm sorry. I know you're upset about Isabella."

"Yeah. She's lying unconscious in a hospital bed, and you guys can't find the creep who did this to her almost two days ago."

"*Us* guys?" Nick protested. "Hey. I'm on a leave of absence, remember? I'm not the one assigned to this case."

"Well, you should be," Jessica snapped.

"The guys are doing their best," Nick said quietly. "They'll find him."

"Oh yeah?"

"Yeah."

Jessica clicked Nick's TV off with the remote control. "They won't, and you know it. Anyway, Dub doesn't have what it takes."

Nick looked back down at his catalog and was

silent for a few moments. "Dub is a fine detective."

"He's got a gut a mile wide," Jessica pointed out. "He doesn't have it in him to chase a little stud like Clay DiPalma."

Nick looked up. His mouth tensed, and his eyes seemed to burn with distant thoughts.

Jessica narrowed her eyes. "Clay DiPalma is probably working his charms right this very minute. . . ."

"Come on, Jess."

"It's true."

Nick closed his book, and Jessica watched as his jaw began to tense with anger. "What I wonder is, what goes through the mind of a guy like Clay DiPalma?"

"What do you mean?" Jessica asked innocently. Nick was definitely starting to pay attention. All she had to do now was help guide his thoughts in the right direction.

"I mean, what's this guy really after?" Nick wondered out loud. "Does he actually think that someone like Isabella would get off on this drug, then come back begging for more? Did he think he was going to land a big new paying customer?"

"Right. People just love having bizarre hallucinations when they go to parties," Jessica said sarcastically. "It really perks up their social skills."

Nick shook his head. "It's sick. I think he just wanted to see her freak out. He's probably the kind of person who tortured cats for kicks when he was in kindergarten."

"You can't let him get away with it," Jessica prodded him.

"But it's not my case," Nick argued. "It's in Dub's hands. He's the detective assigned to it."

Jessica straightened and looked him in the eye. "Yes, but you've got to *make* it your business. You're the only detective in this town who is smart enough to sting this guy."

"Sting?" Nick repeated, his eyes opening wide. "I hope you're not thinking what I think you're thinking. . . ."

Jessica held up her chin. "It's the right thing to do."

"I'm on a leave of absence, Jess. I want to retire from the police force and get my law degree, an office with a window, and maybe a little house on the corner with a white picket fence. I want to live my life like everyone else."

"You're not like everyone else," Jessica argued.

"I don't need that stuff anymore."

Jessica jumped up off the sofa. "But people need *you!*"

Nick held up his hands. "Whoa!"

Jessica felt her heart unexpectedly speed up. Hot tears welled up in her eyes. She pointed a glossy nail at Nick's chest. "How can you *sit* there, staring at university course descriptions, while Isabella is *dying* and the drug dealer who did this to her is running around Sweet Valley looking for more victims?"

"Come on, Jess. . . ."

Jessica crossed her arms. "You are going to go out there and *sting* that guy."

"Jessica . . ."

"For Isabella's sake and for mine," Jessica insisted.

Nick shrugged helplessly. "But I wouldn't even know where to find him."

"Talk to the guys over at Alpha Chi," Jessica suggested, crawling back over to Nick's side. She snuggled next to him and began a series of little kisses that climbed up his neck and ended at his ear. "Someone must have tipped him off to the party. Someone must have at least talked to him. That fraternity house is probably *crawling* with clues."

Nick's jaw tensed.

Jessica smiled. She saw what was in Nick's heart, even if he couldn't see it himself.

Chapter
Twelve

"Now what?" Nick paced in front of his tiny apartment fireplace. He stuffed his hands in his pockets and tried to think. He realized that he'd been swept into Jessica's outrage over Clay DiPalma. Plus he'd probably given her more encouragement than he'd meant to. After all, he couldn't just act on his own, without the blessing of the police department.

With a deep breath he tried to shake out his tangled thoughts. So far he hadn't dared tell Jessica about his meeting with Artie. His plan had been to go about things quietly, without involving her. The last thing he wanted was to put Jessica in danger again.

Of course anyone could make a citizen's arrest, and he had every reason to do so. Clay DiPalma was an outrage and a real threat to everyone in Sweet Valley. Sure, he could trust the whole thing to Dub Harrison. But Jessica was probably right. Clay was too smart and too fast for Dub.

What was he supposed to do? Just sit there and

wait? Listen to Jessica nag and cajole him for the next few weeks until something happened or until the case faded away into oblivion?

"Thanks, Bill," Jessica was saying. She hung up the phone in Nick's kitchen and turned to him with a huge smile. "Bingo."

"What?"

"I just talked to this Sigma I know named Bill Dupree," Jessica said excitedly. She walked over and cradled Nick's face in her hands. "And he just gave me a great lead. We might find our Clay DiPalma after all."

Nick felt an unexpected pang in his gut. "What does he know?"

Jessica sat down at the kitchen table and crossed her legs. "Well, I remembered seeing Bill talking to Clay during the cocktail party. They were into this really intense conversation out on the front porch."

"OK, OK . . ."

Jessica smiled and let out a soft whistle. "Back into the swing of things again, aren't you?"

"Come on, Jess."

"Anyway," Jessica continued, "Bill said that he and Clay had been comparing notes on their Harley-Davidson bikes. Apparently Clay is a real motorcycle nut, and he was bragging about a new model he just bought down at the dealership."

Nick smiled. "Perfect."

"Uh-huh." Jessica winked. "I guess he bought a superprimo, fully loaded model, totally dripping with chrome and *mucho* power. So Bill asked him if

186

he got a pretty good deal on it, and Clay told him yes and if he wanted to check it out, the guy who sold it to him was a guy named Buddy Lasky."

"You are a genius," Nick said, high fiving Jessica. "Lasky should have his name and address and the serial number of the bike. Everything."

"Call him," Jessica prodded.

"Right," Nick said, pulling his phone book out of a drawer and flipping through the yellow pages. "Here it is, Sweet Valley Harley-Davidson." He punched out the phone number and asked for Buddy Lasky.

"Hello, this is Buddy," a voice answered.

"Yeah," Nick said. "My name is Nick Fox and . . . I'm a law enforcement officer investigating a drug-related crime on the Sweet Valley University campus."

"What can I help you with?"

"Well, a young guy came in there recently and bought a top-of-the-line bike from you, and we're trying to track him down."

"What did he look like?"

"Shoulder-length brown hair, olive skin, dark eyes, tall, lanky build," Nick said. "He could have been wearing his hair in a ponytail."

"Oh yeah," Buddy said instantly. "How could I forget him? I called him Mr. Swagger. Under my breath, of course."

Nick chuckled. "That's him."

"I remember that kid because he was bragging pretty shamelessly about his exploits with the ladies. And he was pretty particular about what he wanted," Buddy explained.

"What did he want?"

"Everything. The works. He didn't seem to have any trouble paying for it either," Buddy said. "And he paid in cash. Can you believe that?"

"Cash, huh?" Nick said. He glanced up at Jessica, who was jumping up and down. "What name did he give you?"

"Let me check," Buddy said. "OK. Here it is. DiPalma. Yeah. Clay DiPalma. You need his address?"

"Sure do."

"OK. Two-four-five-zero West Twenty-sixth Street, apartment B, Sweet Valley. Phone?"

"Shoot."

Nick wrote down the phone number. "Thank you very much, sir." He hung up and smiled at Jessica. "That was the easiest piece of crucial information I've ever picked up in my life."

Jessica puffed on her nails and buffed them on her shirtfront. "You couldn't have done it without yours truly, of course."

Nick slipped his arms around Jessica's slender waist. "Hey, partner."

Jessica gave him her most brilliant smile. "Just like the old days." She extracted herself from his embrace. "Go on. Call him up," she urged.

"Jessica . . ."

"Go on," Jessica challenged him, picking up the phone and pointing to it. "Tell him you and your buddies want a little something for the weekend. For fun."

"Yeah, right."

"Do it," Jessica said, giving him a sultry look.

188

"What's the matter? Don't have it in you anymore?"

"He knows me," Nick argued. "I punched him out, *remember?*"

Jessica smiled. "Exactly."

"Then why would he want to deal with me?"

Jessica punched his chin lightly. "Because he knows you're a real tough guy."

"So?"

Jessica placed her hand on her hip. "What if you'd walked up to him in a blazer that day, shaken his hand like a good little boy, and asked him to please stop molesting your girlfriend? All he'd remember was the diphead preppy who was too frightened to stand up for himself. If you called a few days later and said you wanted angel dust, you'd look totally suspicious. But you charged him like a bad boy. He understands that. In his mind you're on his side."

Nick glared at her and grabbed the phone. "Give me that." He punched in the number and waited. The phone rang several times before a guy answered, "Yeah?"

Nick cleared his throat. "Clay DiPalma?"

There was a pause. "Yeah."

"Nick Fox. We met at the Alpha Chi party on Saturday night. . . ."

"Oh yeah? Who were you with? I don't remember," Clay said cautiously.

Nick hesitated for a moment. "I was with a very beautiful blonde named Jessica Wakefield."

"Oh, *that* Jessica," Clay said slowly.

"You remember us?"

"I remember you guys *before* the party, actually," Clay said. "And I don't like the way you solve your problems with your girlfriend."

"Hey, don't take it personally," Nick said. "I reacted, OK?"

"Uh-huh."

"She and I split up anyway," Nick heard himself say.

Nick heard a gasp from behind. A hand slapped his arm. *Hard*.

"Yeah? How come?" Clay said.

Nick took his time. "Let's just say I didn't like the way she was looking at you."

Clay laughed. "So how did you get my number?"

Nick froze. "I just got it, OK? The person who gave it to me doesn't want to be involved."

Clay broke into a laugh. "So what do you want now, frat boy?"

"Uh, some friends and I are having a little party this weekend," Nick began.

"And what does that have to do with me?" Clay replied.

"Thought you might be able to help us out," Nick said, forcing a nervous tone. "Can you?"

"Depends on what you're after."

"What do you have?" Nick ventured.

"I've got a line on a few things," Clay said cautiously. "You're interested, huh?"

"Sure."

"I might be able to help you out," Clay said.

"Where?"

"I use a house out on White's Boulevard," Clay said. "The number is two twenty-six. It's a one-story white house, and there won't be any lights on, if you know what I mean. Meet me there tomorrow night at eleven."

"Got it," Nick said.

"And bring that Jessica with you," Clay added.

"I'm telling you, man," Nick protested. "We split."

"All the more reason to bring her."

"Forget it. She's got nothing to do with this."

"What do you mean, 'She's got nothing to do with this'?"

"I meant it," Nick said calmly.

"It's got *everything* to do with me!" Jessica shouted. How could Nick be so insensitive? This was her friend lying in the hospital. And she had been the one who'd nearly gotten mixed up with Clay, not Nick. It had absolutely *everything* to do with her.

Nick headed for his closet and lugged out a large black suitcase. He hoisted it up on the kitchen table and snapped it open. "You're not going."

"What do you mean, I'm not going?" Jessica cried. "This was *my idea*."

Nick rummaged through the case, pulled out a small recording device, and shook out the tangled wires. "Then you can just say that you were the brains of the operation and I was the brawn."

"Don't patronize me," Jessica protested. "I want to go. I *have* to go. It's too exciting to miss."

"No way," Nick said, punching the eject button

on his minirecorder. "Clay DiPalma is bad news."

"Of course he's bad news," Jessica said hotly.

Nick turned to face her, his expression serious. "No. I mean *really* bad news."

"He's just a punk!"

Nick stopped rummaging through his bag. He looked straight at her. "Look, Jessica. He's dangerous. I know more about him than I've told you so far."

Jessica's eyes widened. *"What?"*

"Artie helped me check this guy out yesterday, Jess," Nick admitted. "There's a good chance he's connected with an L.A. drug ring. And if that's true, this guy would stop at nothing to protect himself. I don't want you within a mile of that slimeball."

She picked up Nick's college catalog and threw it to the floor. "When I think of all the times I've saved your—"

"Jessica," Nick warned.

"You *need* my help," Jessica said forcefully.

Nick didn't take his eyes off her face. "I can't risk it."

"*You're* the one who can't risk it," Jessica said hotly.

"Anything could happen. . . ."

Jessica's pulse raced with fear and indignation. "Anything could happen to *you* if you take this on yourself. If I don't come, you'll have no backup. *Nada.* And if something goes wrong, you'll be left hanging out to dry, Mr. Big Shot."

"I can handle this," Nick said, his expression softening.

"No squad cars or firepower waiting around the corner to rescue you," Jessica chanted. "No radio contact. No warrant."

Nick sat down weakly.

"In fact," Jessica began in a teasing voice, "I have half a mind to make a phone call down to the precinct—"

"What?"

Jessica gave him an enigmatic gaze. "Yeah. Maybe I'll just give your old boss a call."

"Jess, come on—"

"Oh, please, Mr. Police Chief!" Jessica cried softly in her best helpless-girl voice. "I'm so worried about my boyfriend, Nick Fox! He wants to protect me so *much,* he's planning his very own personal *sting!*"

"You wouldn't." Nick rubbed his neck.

Jessica dropped to her knees. "Oh, please, Mr. Police Chief. Don't let him do it! Won't he get in trouble with you for acting on his own?"

"Oh, man." Nick shook his head. He took Jessica's hands and pulled her back up. "You're too much."

"Plus . . ." Jessica leaned against his heaving chest.

"Plus what?" Nick asked. His green eyes had really softened up, Jessica noticed. And that was *exactly* what she wanted right now.

Jessica let her eyes fill with tears. "Plus . . . I didn't really like your tactics."

"What tactics?"

"I don't see why you had to tell him that we'd

193

broken up," Jessica said in a quavering voice.

"I had to," Nick insisted. "If something goes wrong, I don't want him taking it out on you."

Jessica pulled away and buried her face in her hands. "Yes, but it was so *easy* for you to say that. The words just sort of poured out of your mouth, as if you'd been *practicing*."

"Jess, I had to," Nick murmured, rubbing her back.

"It hurt," Jessica sobbed. "How did you say it? 'We split'? Jeez. I mean, how could you?"

Nick turned and slipped his arms around her. Then, as Jessica turned toward him, he pressed his lips to hers. "Please don't cry."

"I can't help it," Jessica whispered, tears streaming down her face. "I just heard you casually tell a complete stranger over the phone that we *split*. It just sort of hit me, Nick. Like, maybe that's what you want. Maybe you don't want me around. Maybe you don't like it that I take an interest in your work and that I'm strong enough to back you up."

"Stop, stop, stop," Nick soothed, covering her tear-stained face with kisses. "That's not true."

"I don't know," Jessica whimpered. "Maybe you'd rather have a Barbie doll for a girlfriend."

"It's just not true," Nick protested. "I love how we can share so much."

Jessica shook her head and looked away. "It just *kills* me that you can say that."

"Stop it."

"I thought I was a part of your life, but I'm not!"

Nick's face had paled. Deep, worried lines had formed in his forehead. "You are!"

"Then prove it."

Nick's shoulders sagged. "OK. OK, come with me. But you're to stay hidden the entire time. Your sole mission will be to call the station if anything happens to me."

Jessica felt a thrill of victory. Her entire face lit up with joy. "Oh, Nick!" she cried.

"You've got me, Jess," Nick said with the old passion she knew so well and had missed.

Jessica threw her arms around Nick and kissed him. She felt his body pull close. His lips, so firm and soft. She stroked the silky skin of his neck and breathed in the clean smell of his shirt. How could she have ever doubted Nick? He was the most wonderful, exciting, loving boyfriend on the face of the earth. And now, she realized, everything that had brought them together was beginning again.

Chapter Thirteen

"Oh, man," Danny groaned. He flipped through his microbiology textbook lifelessly. "This exam is going to be a killer."

"When is it?" Tom asked. He readjusted the pillow behind his back on the bed.

"Friday," Danny told him. "It covers one hundred and fourteen pages of text. Microbial metabolism, microbial growth, and the functional anatomy of prokaryotic and eukaryotic cells."

"I'm glad I'm a journalism major." Tom shook his head. "There's just no way I could hack that."

Danny shrugged. "There's no way I could put together five news broadcasts a week and carry seventeen credits like you do." He checked his watch. "It's seven o'clock right now. Four hours per night. Four nights before the exam. One hundred fourteen pages, divided by four. That's about twenty-eight . . . that's about seven pages per hour. Not counting the extra reading Jacobson wants me to do."

"Give it a break," Tom muttered. "Are you human or machine?"

"Machine," Danny said grimly.

Tom whistled and bent back down over his laptop.

Danny flopped open his text and stared at the page. Only instead of words, numbers, and graphs, the image of a face began to appear before his eyes. His stomach tightened. It didn't matter where he was or what he was doing, Isabella was always right there with him. Reminding him. Teasing him. Haunting him.

"What would *you* have done?" Danny said suddenly. He turned around in his desk chair.

Tom looked up from his laptop. "Huh?"

"What would you have done if that had been Elizabeth on Saturday night?"

Tom stared. "What are you talking about? I'd be *freaking* right now if Elizabeth were lying in that hospital bed."

Danny waved off his words. "No. I mean, what would you have done if Elizabeth had gone slightly off her gourd that night? You know. Dancing with ten guys at once. Puffing away at who knows what with some guy you've never seen before. Ignoring you . . ."

Tom looked thoughtful. "I don't know."

"Come on, Tombo."

"What can I say?" Tom tried to explain. "It doesn't sound like something Elizabeth would do, but then, nothing's impossible." He frowned. "Hey, I've been known to get toasted at the occasional frat function."

197

He shook his head. "You've seen me flip—"

"Yeah, but we're talking about your girlfriend, not you," Danny snapped.

Tom sighed. "I'd be mad if Elizabeth did that, OK? I'd probably try to figure out what was wrong."

"Yeah, yeah, yeah," Danny said impatiently. He stood up and stomped across the room. "But what if she didn't want to tell you? What if she refuses to listen? What if she trots off with another guy?"

Tom shrugged. "I'd probably let it blow over. But that's not the point."

Danny wanted to tear out his hair. "What are you talking about?"

"What I'm saying," Tom said forcefully, "is that whatever problems you and Isabella were having that night had nothing to do with her accident. That creep could have passed PCP off on anyone at that party."

"It wouldn't have happened if she'd done what I'd told her," Danny burst out.

"Isabella's not your kid," Tom protested. "She's a grown woman."

Danny rubbed his jaw. "You don't understand."

"Yeah, I do," Tom said. "You blame yourself for Isabella's accident because you have this weird and totally irrational idea that you are entirely responsible for her. And you're not, man."

"You've got that right," Danny said angrily.

"Chill," Tom told him. "Get ahold of yourself. Forgive Isabella if you care about her, and get your butt over to that hospital."

Danny spread his arms wide in frustration. "It's not that easy."

"Why aren't you there, man?"

"Because I can't do it!" Danny shouted. He dropped limply back down on his chair. "I'm too crazy. I can't—I don't know. I'm still too angry about it."

Tom shook his head. "I can't help you there."

"I just can't get over it," Danny said. "She was deliberately trying to shock me on Saturday night."

"People say a lot of things when they're angry," Tom said quietly. "It doesn't mean they're true."

Danny sank his head down in his hands.

"Forgive her," Tom said simply.

Danny looked up and shook his head weakly.

"People do things they regret," Tom said in a quiet, halting voice. For a moment Tom paused as if he were unable to go on. "They need forgiveness from the people they love."

"I can't pretend. . . ."

"Yeah, but it's eating you up inside," Tom said. "You're going nowhere with this. Look at yourself."

Danny clenched his teeth and spun around. He pulled his microbiology text in front of him and stared hard at it. He had to get over this. He had to forget Isabella. He couldn't be this angry. It would destroy him.

I've got to get on with my life, Danny told himself, shutting his textbook and pulling out his green microbiology notebook instead, which was stacked with several other class notebooks on his desk. But as he lifted it out, several unfamiliar papers suddenly slipped onto the floor. Danny picked them up and stared. There were four pages altogether, printed and stapled.

Danny felt a strange twisting in his stomach. Slowly, as he looked at the pages, he began to realize that what he was holding was a microbiology exam. At the top of the first page he saw Professor Jacobson's name. Then alongside her name was Friday's date. The date of the very exam he was studying for.

"Did you know that Woodward and Bernstein never revealed their main source for the Watergate break-in story?" Elizabeth said.

Tom nodded. "Deep Throat."

"It's incredible that it's never come out."

Tom glanced up from his laptop. "If that had happened today, Deep Throat would collect a six-figure advance on a tell-all book."

"And make the talk-show rounds."

"Shhh."

Elizabeth looked up. Though she and Tom had sprawled themselves out in an obscure hall of the library's third floor, near the Western Reading Room, a wandering librarian was glaring steadily at them from the nearby stacks.

"Back to journalism case studies," Elizabeth muttered under her breath.

"Back to my American history paper," Tom whispered, playfully nudging her in the side. After a moment he asked, "Would *you* take the six-figure advance?"

She smiled and shook her head.

"Me neither."

Elizabeth watched Tom as he hunched over and typed. The side of his thigh bumped against her, sending her heart into unexpected double time. Elizabeth took in every tiny detail of his appearance, from his unruly dark hair to his faded green T-shirt to the worn leather watchband he always wore on his muscular forearm. He frowned at the screen, then punched the delete button quickly and began rewriting.

"Almost done?" she couldn't resist saying.

Tom stared at the opposite wall, then turned and smiled. "I'd be done now if you weren't in such a chatty mood."

Elizabeth laughed, then bit her bottom lip. "I'm sorry. I can't help it. I just want to talk."

Tom kept typing and shaking his head. "Chatty, chatty, chatty."

"That's what I missed most when I was away from you," Elizabeth said shyly.

"What?"

"Just talking."

Tom looked up. He set his laptop down. Then he glanced over to the stacks for a quick check on the librarian, who had disappeared. He slipped his arms around Elizabeth's waist and turned her toward him.

"Tom," Elizabeth whispered with longing before he touched his lips to hers.

Elizabeth shifted and wrapped her arms around his neck, pulling him closer as the kiss intensified. For a very long moment Elizabeth forgot everything. The library. The case studies. All she could think about was the swell of feelings Tom stirred inside her. For a moment she was sure she was going to cry.

"Talking is all you missed?" Tom asked her, breathless as he pulled his lips away from hers.

Elizabeth drew in a deep, quavering breath, then let it out again. "You know what I mean, Tom. We talk. But it's not just that we're talking. We're talking about things we *want* to talk about. We don't have to fake it."

"Nope," Tom said. He smiled and shook his head a little and playfully patted his cheeks, still recovering from their kiss.

"Am I distracting you?" Elizabeth teased.

Tom smiled ruefully at his laptop screen. "Oh yeah." He pressed the return button several times and frowned.

Elizabeth looked off dreamily. "Talking."

"Talking," Tom echoed back absently.

"Yeah," Elizabeth said. "It's not that easy with a lot of people. I mean with Scott Sinclair, it was completely different."

"Not him again," Tom said, punching his keyboard rapidly, then stopping. He stared and bit his thumbnail.

"I'm just using him as an example," Elizabeth told him. "I mean, he wanted to talk about journalism and the *Gazette* and everything. But he was so *serious* and egotistical about it."

"I bet he was."

Elizabeth stretched out her arms. "With you I can say anything, and it's OK. We share ideas. You listen. . . ."

"I'm not listening—I'm trying to finish this." Tom turned to flip through a book at his side.

"Or you laugh," Elizabeth went on dreamily. She closed her book and cuddled up next to him. "Did you have that same problem with Dana Upshaw?"

Tom's body suddenly seized up. "What problem?"

"The *problem*," Elizabeth repeated, "of not really clicking. Talking, but not really talking about what you want to talk about."

"I'm sorry," Tom said curtly, looking away. "I don't know what you're getting at."

Elizabeth's face fell. "All I was asking was—"

Tom closed his document and shut his laptop. "Let's go. I can't concentrate."

Elizabeth grabbed his arm. "Wait a minute. What's going on?"

"Nothing," Tom said, pulling away. He shoved his book in his pack and began buckling it shut.

Elizabeth let out a short, exasperated laugh. "I don't believe this."

"What?"

Elizabeth stuck her book under her arm and stood up with him. "We were having a perfectly fine study session until I started talking about Scott Sinclair and Dana Upshaw."

Tom hoisted his backpack over his shoulder. "I guess I'm just a little tired, that's all."

"That's not it," Elizabeth came back. "Something's bothering you. What's going on? Look, I told you. Scott Sinclair is out of my life *forever.* Just thinking about how involved I got with that guy makes me sick. Don't you understand that?"

"Yeah. I understand," Tom said dully as they headed down the hall toward the main library staircase.

"Then—then why are you acting so distant all of a sudden?" Elizabeth whispered loudly.

"It's nothing," Tom said, pushing open the library's front glass door and holding it for Elizabeth.

Elizabeth stomped out. Then she stopped and turned to face him. "That's not true. It's not *nothing*. You just don't want to talk about what we did when we were apart. And I don't think that's right."

Tom brushed by her and headed for the steps. "Can't we just put the past behind us?"

Elizabeth hurried stubbornly ahead. "It's *not* in the past yet. It's obviously not sorted out. I mean, it hurts sometimes to talk about the past, but I don't want to tiptoe around it anymore. I don't want to live like that. I want openness and honesty. I got this weird e-mail today and it got me thinking—"

Tom stopped. "Why are you doing this?" he asked her. His eyes flashed angrily. "Why is it so important to you? Why do we have to keep rehashing this junk?"

"Because I don't want to go back to the way we were!" Elizabeth cried. She ignored the stares of the late night study owls walking past them on the library steps.

"I do!"

"But don't you understand?" Elizabeth cried. "We broke up because we weren't honest with each other. We didn't trust."

"Can we talk about this tomorrow?" Tom said, his eyes darting nervously.

Elizabeth opened her mouth to speak, then stopped herself. She followed Tom silently down the library's front steps, along the grass-lined quad walkway, and out toward the wide path leading to the dorms. The night air was soft, and the flickering yellow lights from Dickenson Hall shone against the darkness. Still, Elizabeth felt as if a heavy curtain had been dropped between her and Tom.

He really doesn't get it, Elizabeth thought sadly. *And I'm not getting through to him because I don't know how to say it.*

She felt a terrifying clutch in her chest. Maybe Tom didn't understand because it just wasn't in his nature. Maybe he'd never be able to trust and to be completely honest with others.

Elizabeth felt as if her heart were breaking in two. After all that it took to get back together, she was beginning to feel as if they never had. The old problems were heading right back like a distant train racing down the track toward them.

*　　　*　　　*

"Sorry I'm so out of it," Tom said.

Elizabeth seemed to stiffen at his side as they walked together along the path that led from the library to the dorms. Up ahead, the lights of Dickenson Hall shone against the black night. Tom slipped his hand into hers.

Elizabeth looked up at him. Her blue-green eyes were troubled. Strands of blond hair blew in her face.

Tom cleared his throat. "I just didn't feel like talking back there."

Elizabeth nodded silently. Tom could feel the tension between them rise up like thick smoke.

He bit his lip and squeezed Elizabeth's hand. "Were you trying to tell me about some weird e-mail you got?"

"Yeah," Elizabeth said quietly. "It was pretty amazing, actually. Scott Sinclair got kicked out of DCIR."

Tom felt some of the heaviness lift from his chest. "Whoa."

"One of his co-reporters did her own little internal investigation on Scott, then wrote a story about it for the paper," Elizabeth explained. "Turns out Scott doctored his transcripts to get into the program."

"No way!" Tom cried, his spirits lifting even more.

"Yeah, and it turned out he had a pattern of sort of wooing women writers." Elizabeth looked up at him with a sad smile. "Like me."

Tom hugged her sideways. "Come on, Liz."

"And once he reeled them in, he used them to do his writing and research."

"What a jerk."

Elizabeth made two fists and held them up angrily. "I can't believe I got sucked into his—his little *scheme*. I feel like such a fool."

"You're not," Tom soothed. He looked off into the dark field to his right. It was true that Elizabeth had been unwittingly pulled into Scott Sinclair's fraud. But it was also true that Scott couldn't have picked anyone more talented and dedicated than Elizabeth.

And if she'd fallen for Scott Sinclair, Tom thought miserably, he had only himself to blame. He'd been the one to unfairly accuse Elizabeth of lying about his father's advances. He'd been the one to break up their relationship over it. And he'd been the one to flaunt his involvement with Dana Upshaw.

What was Elizabeth supposed to do? Curl up and die?

Tom stopped at the front door to Elizabeth's dorm and kissed her gently on the cheek. It was painful to see her face so cool and full of pain. He knew that she wanted him to open up. But he couldn't talk to her right now about why he couldn't. It was just too painful. He wasn't ready to talk. But he knew deep down that things couldn't go on this way forever. . . .

Chapter Fourteen

I'll be glad when this *is over*, Danny told himself as he hurried into the elevator in the biosciences building. He knew that Professor Jacobson arrived at her office like clockwork every morning at seven forty-five. If he caught her at just the right moment, before she was interrupted by phone calls and student meetings, he'd have a chance to return the exam, explain the mix-up, and be out of there in a jiffy. Sure, Jacobson was a top professor, but she was *not* a person Danny wanted to spend personal time with.

When the elevator opened, Danny turned right and headed down the hallway. But as he approached her frosted glass office door he slowed. For a brief instant he closed his eyes and mentally practiced telling her how he'd accidentally picked up the exam.

"Wyatt!" a sharp voice interrupted his thoughts. "You're sleeping on your feet in my hallway!"

Danny's eyes flew open. Professor Jacobson had

pushed open her door and was standing in front of him, glaring. He winced inwardly. The professor's green suit and sprayed helmet of hair always made him think of army drill sergeants and military tanks.

"OK," she said tiredly, pushing open her door and ushering him in. "What do you want from me?"

Danny forced himself to be calm. After all, he'd picked up the exam accidentally. He was doing the honorable thing and bringing it back immediately. Why would Professor Jacobson have any problem with that?

"Uh, Professor . . . ," Danny began.

"What is it, Wyatt? Spit it out. I've got class in five minutes."

Danny handed her the exam. "I set my notebook down on your desk yesterday when we were talking after class. I guess I picked this up accidentally when I left."

Professor Jacobson looked at the exam in horror. "What?"

"I'm sorry," Danny stammered. "I discovered it last night. So this is the very first chance I've had to return it and get this problem sorted—"

"This *problem?*" Professor Jacobson cried. She snapped the exam with the back of her hand. Then she turned away and marched over to her desk. "This is an *outrage.*"

Danny felt his knees buckle. "It was an accident. I'm bringing the exam *back.* I didn't even look at it."

"Mr. Wyatt," the professor said tartly, "I've heard plenty of stories in my thirty years of university teaching. But this takes the cake."

"Takes the what?"

"It was an accident," Professor Jacobson mimicked sarcastically.

Danny's eyes opened wide. *"Yes."*

"Do you know how long it took me to prepare that examination?" A red flush crept up the professor's wrinkled cheeks. "Do you know how long I searched my classroom, lab, and office last night looking for it?"

"Professor Jacobson, you've got it all wrong. . . ."

"And even after I go to all the trouble of rewriting this examination, you still will be familiar with the focus of my questions," she rattled on. "And I do not wish to change the focus. These are the areas I believe are critical to the class's understanding of the material."

"But it was an accident," Danny said weakly. "I—I don't know what else to say—"

"Don't bother. I don't believe you, Wyatt."

Danny stared at her in disbelief.

She checked her watch and picked up her briefcase. "We'll have to discuss this later today. I don't have time for this right now."

"I didn't steal the exam," Danny protested as she rushed past him.

"I have several options at my disposal," she said sharply. "I can fail you for Friday's exam right now for cheating. I can fail you for the entire semester. Or I can notify the dean's office for more extensive disciplinary action."

"You can't be serious!"

"I'll listen to you *later*, Mr. Wyatt," Professor Jacobson said over her shoulder.

Something stuck in Danny's throat. For a moment he thought he was about to choke. As he watched Professor Jacobson stalk out of her office he saw his whole life slipping away with her. Fail microbiology? Face down the dean on charges of cheating?

We're talking extreme dip in the GPA, Danny told himself. *We're looking at five wasted months in class time. We're talking good-bye grad school. And why?*

Danny thought back. It had been Monday when Jacobson called him to her lab desk. He'd been distracted and upset about Isabella's accident when he must have picked up the exam. He just hadn't been thinking straight. He'd been thinking about Isabella.

Isabella again.

Way to go, Izzy, Danny thought venomously. *Thanks to you, my whole life is going down the drain.*

"Fresh batteries in your tape recorder?" Jessica whispered.

"Yep," Nick said quickly, stuffing a wire into his jeans pocket and patting it.

"Think he's in there yet?" Jessica lifted her head and peeked through the window of Nick's Camaro. They were parked on White's Boulevard, a long stretch of road out of town, dotted with farmhouses, scraggly palm trees, and miles of empty fields. Across the street Jessica could barely make out the dark outline of the dilapidated white house Clay DiPalma had described for his rendezvous with Nick.

"I'm going in," Nick whispered. "It's just before eleven."

"Look," Jessica said, lifting up again from her crouched position in the backseat as headlights swept the inside of the car. "Someone's coming."

"OK," Nick murmured. "I'm going to let him go inside first."

Jessica watched as a dark sports car pulled up into the driveway next to the house. The car lights flicked off. A moment later she saw the car door open and the lanky figure of a young man step out onto the driveway. For a moment he paused. He slipped his hands into his pockets and rocked back and forth on his heels.

"There he is," Nick said. "He's alone."

Jessica watched Clay move into the shadows at the side of the building.

"Stay here," Nick told her.

Jessica grabbed his arm. "Are you kidding? You *need* me over there."

"I've changed my mind. I don't want DiPalma to know you're here," Nick argued. "If he finds out, he'll know I was lying."

Jessica's eyes blazed. "We already agreed. You need backup."

Nick looked away and rubbed his chin. Then he looked into her eyes intently. "Wait here for exactly two minutes. If you don't hear anything, I want you to walk over to the other side of the house and find a spot where you can't be seen but you'll be able to hear anything going on inside."

"Right," Jessica whispered back.

"You OK?"

Jessica felt her heart speed up. "Oh yeah."

Nick gave her a long look. "Keep your fingers crossed."

Jessica swallowed hard. She looked at the slight stubble on Nick's chin and the intense concentration in his eyes as he watched the house. And all at once she realized how much was at stake. If things didn't go smoothly, the entire Sweet Valley police force would be on his back. Yet Nick had the best chance of pulling off the scheme. He was faster and smarter than his old colleagues, and he knew it.

Still, Jessica thought with a shiver, *we have no backup*. If anything went wrong, no one would spring out from behind the bushes to rescue them. No one even knew they were there.

When Nick was sure that Jessica was well concealed in the backseat, he slipped out of the car and jogged across the road toward the house.

Earlier he'd strapped a small revolver to his side, right under his baggy sweatshirt. His miniature tape recorder was taped carefully to his thigh, and a wire snaked up his back so that its tiny mike was concealed beneath his neckline.

On the outside he knew he looked like a typical

frat boy, right down to the baseball cap and basketball shoes. He stuffed his hands into his pockets and tried to walk like a casual jock.

It was a clear night. The moonlight streamed against the side of the house, illuminating the boarded-up windows, collapsed front porch, and peeling paint. When Nick tried the small door on the right side of the house, it opened easily. He pushed it open all the way before walking in, his eyes peeled for danger. "Anyone here?" he called out.

"Yo."

Nick stepped carefully forward. The doorway led into a dilapidated kitchen. An ancient refrigerator stood with its door hanging halfway off. Two of the lower cabinets had been kicked in. A mouse scuttled across the crumbling floor.

A small light clicked on. Nick blinked. Clay DiPalma stood in a narrow hallway that led into the kitchen from the other side of the house. He was wearing black jeans and a hooded black sweatshirt. His hands were bunched up inside its front pocket. Nick eyed the pocket carefully.

"Have any trouble?" Clay asked.

Nick shook his head. The temptation to take Clay out was pretty brutal, but he held himself in check. He reminded himself that he was playing the part of an innocent frat boy looking for a few kicks. He told himself to be slightly nervous yet ready to play tough, the way Clay DiPalma probably expected him to be. "No. Everything was fine."

"OK," Clay said cautiously. He stepped forward and looked Nick up and down.

"So . . . uh, how much does this stuff cost?" Nick asked.

"Depends."

"Depends on what?" Nick crossed his arms nervously.

"Depends on what you want and how much."

"Oh. Well, me and a few of the guys just want a few hits of angel dust for a party we're having this weekend," Nick said with a shrug.

"You like that stuff, huh?" Clay leaned up against the broken stove.

"Well, uh, actually I've—we've—never tried it before," Nick said.

"Oh. Right," Clay said. "They say you can see all kinds of strange things on angel dust. Things you wouldn't believe."

"Yeah. It's like that, I guess," Nick said, digging his hands into his front pockets. "So. What do you want for six hits?"

"But I don't know what you're talking about," Clay said in a mocking voice.

Nick tensed. "What?"

"I don't know what you're talking about," Clay repeated.

Nick felt sick. "I don't understand. . . ."

Clay suddenly threw back his head and began laughing.

"Hey, what's so funny?" Nick demanded.

But Clay didn't stop laughing. The guy staggered

backward, holding his stomach and gasping for breath. "Oh, man, you're too much."

"Dude, what's your problem?" Nick protested. "Let's get this over with. OK?"

Clay pointed at Nick. "You crack me up, man."

Nick looked around nervously.

"I really like your nasty frat boy disguise," Clay drawled. "You really thought I'd go for it, didn't you? You cops are all alike. Dumb as fence posts."

Nick stiffened. He watched as Clay swaggered toward him, his hands moving beneath his sweatshirt.

"Take it easy," Nick said slowly, holding up his hands.

"Ha!" Clay teased. "Not sure what I've got under here, are you?"

"Come on, man," Nick said. "Let's talk things over."

Clay looked over his shoulder and grinned. "Hey. I bet you brought your girlfriend after all."

"No," Nick said calmly, though his heart was pumping double time. *Where are you, Jessica?* he thought desperately. *Stay away. Just stay away.*

Without breaking his lock on Nick's gaze, Clay swiftly drew a gun out from under his sweatshirt and aimed it directly at him. "What's the matter? Smart cop got nothing to say?"

Nick looked at him closely. Clay's upper lip was beaded with sweat. He was shaking slightly, and his pupils were dilated. Nick knew that Clay was probably on something. Maybe hallucinating. Maybe he was seeing a rabid beast in front of him instead of a man. If he spotted Jessica, he might see her as anything—a panther, a poisonous snake, a giant scorpion. Who knew what was going through his mind? And why *wouldn't* Clay shoot at them? If he was high, he'd think he was defending himself.

Nick stood still and tried to think fast. But all he could think about was how bringing Jessica along had turned into a huge mistake. Right now she was probably a few feet away. Practically in point-blank range.

Jessica slunk back down onto the backseat. She twisted her blond hair on top of her head and slipped on a black knit cap.

"That's two minutes, Nick," she whispered, patting her jacket. In its inner pocket was a tiny flashlight, a can of pepper spray, a portable alarm, and a small cell phone.

She lifted her head an inch so that she could peek out the window. "Here goes."

Slowly Jessica opened the back door of the car, slipped out, shut it quietly, and crouched down in the darkness of the road. She hurried across the empty street and made her way to a clump of overgrown bushes along the left side of the house.

"Done," she muttered.

She closed her eyes as she pushed through the dusty, prickly branches. A cobweb attached itself to her mouth. A nail sticking out of the building scratched her arm. Jessica moved ahead on her hands and knees until she reached the first side window. From there she hoped she could hear what was going on inside.

"Ouch," Jessica whispered to herself as a branch scraped her cheek. Broken glass began to crunch noisily beneath her feet. She stopped and looked up. She was right under the window. And it had already been smashed open.

Slowly Jessica raised herself up from her crouched position. She prayed that she could get a glimpse inside without Clay detecting her there.

Go, Jessica told herself.

She popped up her head and quickly took in the room. Luckily she was able to make out a few things. A tiny stream of light from the other side of the house filtered through the hallway opposite her. The room was empty except for an overturned sofa shoved up against one wall, scattered cardboard boxes, and a pile of garbage in the fireplace.

After she ducked back down again, she began to hear the quiet murmur of voices. From what she could tell, only Clay and Nick were inside. But she couldn't be sure. Slowly and carefully she straightened up and peeked again through the window. But as soon as she did she dropped back down again. Nick and Clay were talking in the kitchen on the other side of the house. She had clearly seen them at the end of the hallway.

She drew her breath sharply. Clay was definitely close enough to hear her slightest noise. It was important to stay perfectly still. The back of her neck prickled with fear.

Please be OK, Nick, Jessica prayed.

A dank smell rose up from a pile of rotting boards next to her feet. She listened as Nick's low voice volleyed with Clay's high-pitched one. Back and forth they went, and the longer they talked, the louder their voices were becoming.

Jessica's eyes opened wide—too wide for tears, though she could feel them building up. This whole conversation didn't sound right. Not right at all. Nick was supposed to take it nice and easy. All he needed to do was buy the dope, give Clay the money, and get it all on tape for the police.

But that wasn't happening.

Jessica bit her knuckle in desperation as the voices rose and grew sharp, echoing off the bare, filthy walls.

Her face burning, she began to tremble. But she held her position under the window. The only thing that saved her from bolting was the thought that she could—as a last resort—use the cell phone to call the police. That was what Nick needed her there for. And this was where she would stay, no matter what. For Nick's sake. For Isabella's sake.

"What is that wonderful smell?" Elizabeth said dreamily as she looked up from her Dylan Thomas book.

"Beef burgundy," Tom replied, flourishing his wooden spoon over the metal pot on his tiny portable hot plate.

Elizabeth giggled. "Are you kidding? You're making beef burgundy on your *desk?*"

"Yep," Tom assured her, opening the small refrigerator under his desk and pulling out a packet of stew meat. "You're smelling freshly minced garlic sautéing in olive oil right now. Next I add the meat. . . ."

"Whoa!" Elizabeth put down her book and got up. Truthfully, she was so overjoyed by Tom's relaxed mood, she couldn't have cared less what they ate. After class that afternoon she'd found a note from Tom slipped under her door. In the message he'd apologized for his behavior at the library the night before and offered to make dinner—and make up.

Tom stirred the meat briskly, then handed Elizabeth the spoon. "Would you stir for a moment, please, while I open two cans of beef broth?"

"Absolutely."

Tom flicked a dishcloth over his shoulder and grinned at her as he opened the cans. "This gourmet creation will simmer gently for an hour."

Elizabeth stirred the sizzling meat. "Mmm."

"Then I will add sliced carrots, potato chunks, and, of course, mushrooms," Tom explained.

"I'm in heaven," Elizabeth said as Tom took the spoon from her hand and adjusted the burner.

"Good," Tom said. "Now go lie down and read your book."

"Yes, sir," Elizabeth said, snuggling back down on Tom's bed and finding her place in the book. "You have my complete obedience now."

"Oooh," Tom teased. "That's a first."

"We have candles too," Elizabeth remembered. "They're in one of your desk drawers."

"Candlelit dinner, huh?" Tom muttered. "Let's just hope Danny decided to spend the evening in the library, where he belongs."

Elizabeth narrowed her eyes. "Has he gone back to see Isabella?"

Tom shook his head. "He's too upset."

Elizabeth shut her book. "Too upset? Well, we're *all* upset. But that doesn't mean we're totally ignoring her."

Tom poured the canned broth into the pot, sending up a cloud of steam. "He's shut down."

"I can't believe it."

"Believe it," Tom said, hoisting himself up on his desk next to the hot plate. He looked down at the stew and stirred it. "Somewhere along the line Danny got the idea that Isabella was his to control."

"And he didn't have control on Saturday night."

"So now he blames himself."

Elizabeth stared at the ceiling. "So if he feels so guilty, why isn't he with her?"

"I guess he's . . . angry with her," Tom explained. "After all, Isabella *did* go off with that guy. He said he tried to rein her in, but . . ."

"Isabella was never perfect enough for Danny," Elizabeth murmured, adding a note of sarcasm.

"Maybe you're right," Tom said softly.

Maybe I'm not, Elizabeth thought. She couldn't understand how Danny could have the nerve to be angry at Isabella while she lay near death in the hospital. Sometimes the male mind worked in mysterious ways. Ways Elizabeth could never understand—or want to.

She stood up, trying to shake away her thoughts of Danny and Isabella. She found two candles in Tom's top desk drawer, lit them, and turned off the harsh fluorescent lights. She lay back down on Tom's bed and watched the yellow light flickering on the ceiling.

"You want to talk about last night," Tom suddenly said. "Don't you?"

Elizabeth looked up. "Yes."

"I'm sorry I was weird," Tom said, his brown eyes thoughtful. "I was just burned out from all the work I've been doing at the station. And then there was that paper I was working on. . . ."

Elizabeth bit her lip guiltily.

Tom rubbed the back of his neck. "And—look, Elizabeth—it's just really hard for me to talk about, you know, other relationships we've had. I'm sorry. I know you want me to be more open, but some things are just . . ."

Elizabeth stood up and rushed over. She hugged him around the waist. "I know. I know."

Tom kissed her tenderly. "Elizabeth . . . I just want us to be together. You have no idea. . . ."

"I do," Elizabeth breathed. "I just get so scared sometimes."

"About what?"

Elizabeth's eyes grew damp. "Scared of losing you all over again."

Tom brushed his lips against hers. "You won't."

"After . . . everything we've been through," Elizabeth said, struggling not to cry, "I just couldn't take it if . . ."

"I couldn't either."

"If you could just let me know . . . somehow . . . that you're opening up to me," Elizabeth begged. "Because I'm trying so hard to be open with you, and it's not easy. I—I don't want to go back to the old Tom and Elizabeth."

"I'll open up to you, Liz. And we won't go back," Tom vowed. He cupped Elizabeth's face in his hands and kissed her again. "I promise."

Oh no, Jessica thought, clamping her hand over her mouth. *Clay knows Nick's a cop. He must!*

Through the side wall of the house she could hear laughter, then a sickening silence, followed by Nick's low voice. Sharp words followed, then only muffled sounds.

Jessica dug her heels into the soft dirt and rocked back and forth in terror. Her instincts told her to spring up out of her hiding place and rush into the house.

But she promised Nick she wouldn't.

Jessica forced herself to be calm. Nick was a trained undercover cop. He had years of experience in stings exactly like this one, and he knew how to get out when he had to.

But he's always worked with a partner! Jessica thought desperately. If she didn't help him, he'd be totally on his own for the first time.

Jessica raised herself up so that her ear was close

to the broken window. She could hear Clay's staccato voice, followed by Nick's deep, reassuring one. The voices seemed to swing back and forth until they were suddenly loud enough to make out.

". . . mess with me," Clay screamed.

"You've got it all wrong," Nick said calmly. "You're making a mistake."

"Oh, I am, am I?" Clay sneered.

"Hey, if you've got a problem with this," Nick was murmuring, "we can just walk away."

Clay let out a weird, high-pitched laugh, and Jessica slipped her hand toward the cell phone in her jacket. Help was just a phone call away, but if she made a move or sound, there was a good chance Clay would hear her.

". . . call the whole thing off now," Nick said.

"Walk *away*? Call it *off*?" Clay screamed. "I've got this pretty-boy *cop* breathing down my neck, and you think I'm going to *take off and forget about it?*"

Jessica let out a soft cry, then muffled it with her hands.

"Come on, man," Nick said. "Chill."

Get out of there, Nick. Get out of there.

"The problem with you freaks is that you're too stupid," Clay yelled. "You can't compete with us, can you? Why don't you just give up?"

"Wait—no!"

Jessica heard a horrifying thump, a grunt, and the heavy, sickening sound of a body hitting the floor.

Unable to hold back another second, Jessica

sprang to her feet and looked through the broken glass just above her head. The light was dim inside, but she could see that Nick was on the floor, sprawled on his side.

Clay, gripping the muzzle of his gun, stared down at Nick's still body. For a moment he seemed to relax, as if he were about to turn away and leave. But then he spun the revolver around in his hand so that it was pointed at Nick.

"Whoo!" Clay stepped over Nick's body and did a little dance.

Jessica stared in horror. Clay's wild eyes were glazed over. In one swift motion he used his free hand to pull Nick's gun out from under his sweatshirt. Then, after shoving the gun across the floor to the opposite wall, he ripped Nick's tape recorder and wires off his body.

"I am so *good!*" he sang out. He clicked open the recorder with his thumb and pocketed the tape.

Oh no. Nick's out cold . . .

"I just want to ce-le-brate!"

. . . and Clay's totally high.

"I am so beau-ti-ful!" Clay shouted, waving his gun in the air.

Jessica couldn't move.

"Hey." Clay suddenly halted in the middle of his crazy dance. His face grew serious. "Wait a minute. I don't think I like your face."

No.

"I don't like cops. And I don't like their faces."

Please, no.

225

Clay spun the revolver in his hand. "Hey, you're going to get what's coming to you sooner or later, *cop*. So why don't we just do the damage now? Huh?"

Jessica let out a gasp. For an instant she was sure Clay heard her.

"I taught the same lesson to Steve Riviera," Clay rambled on. "A better cop than you'll *ever* be, Fox."

Jessica felt her knees shake. She ran her tongue over her dry lips and swallowed hard.

Clay stood perfectly still, his gun pointed directly at Nick's head. His eyes glittered as he sang softly, "And now . . . it's time . . . to say . . . good-bye. . . ."

Chapter
Fifteen

"I've never eaten so much in my entire life." Elizabeth groaned happily. She stretched out on Tom's bed, an empty plate of beef burgundy on her stomach, her legs draped over Tom's.

"It was the red wine," Tom said.

Elizabeth laughed. "How much did you put in?"

"I stopped counting after four cups."

Elizabeth gave him a playful slap.

"Anyway," Tom said. "It wasn't the wine. It was the company."

"Sometimes I wish we could just forget everything and run away for a while," Elizabeth said.

"Not forever?" Tom pretended to look hurt.

"No," Elizabeth said, setting her dish down on the floor. She stretched her arms up languidly above her head. "Just for a while. I'd like to go somewhere and pretend that we were the only two people in the world. Maybe a lovely island in the South Seas."

"No news to cover. No friends in trouble. No class," Tom joined in.

"No class?" Elizabeth joked. "Hey!"

"You know what I mean."

Elizabeth drifted away in thought. "Do you think that would be boring?"

Tom laughed. "I could do it."

Elizabeth nodded. "Two weeks."

"Four weeks," Tom said, staring out the window.

"When's Danny coming back?" Elizabeth murmured, stroking the side of Tom's arm.

"I don't know," Tom said. He leaned over and kissed her. "Why don't we clean up here and go for a walk?"

"OK. Then I have to put in an hour down at the *Gazette*," Elizabeth told him. "I promised Ed I'd write a quick story from an admissions office press release."

"Don't go away," Tom said, lifting her legs and standing up. "I'm going to rinse these dishes off in the bathroom."

"OK," Elizabeth agreed.

Elizabeth stretched out happily as Tom backed out the door with the dishes. She breathed in the scent of him on his sheets. What was it? Soap? Aftershave? The smell of clean cotton? She didn't even want to analyze it. Her whole body was floating with contentment.

She stared lovingly at the bulletin board above his bed, a jumble of newspaper clippings, journalism awards, editorial cartoons, ticket stubs, and photographs.

228

Just then she caught a glimpse of a photograph that had been taken of her and Tom together at the beach several months before. In the picture Tom was blowing a big gum bubble and crossing his eyes. She was looking at him, her head thrown back in a huge smile. Behind them the ocean seemed to stretch out forever.

Elizabeth grinned. The photo reminded her of so many things Tom had given her. The fun. The talks. The work. The crazy times. Sometimes it seemed as if she and Tom had climbed every mountain and crossed every sea together. The bonds between them were so strong, she didn't believe that anything could ever tear them apart again.

She instinctively reached up to touch the image. But just as she did, the photo's rusty tack loosened from the cork board.

"Whoops!" Elizabeth grabbed for it just as it slipped between the wall and the bed. She reached down and groped the floor with her fingertips until her hand suddenly bumped against something.

"Mmm," Elizabeth murmured, pulling up the object. She sat up cross-legged and turned it around in her hands. It was a small, blue cardboard package with black-and-white lettering.

Elizabeth stared hard at the box. "Condoms," she said dully. *"Condoms?"*

Elizabeth flipped over the box in a daze, as if its fine print held some kind of explanation. What was Tom doing with condoms? They hadn't taken that step yet. So why had he . . . ?

Her fingers slipped numbly under the broken cardboard seal. Inside, she saw that the condoms were packaged in sheets. She shook them out lightly onto her hand. Three sheets. Four foil-wrapped condoms to a sheet. Twelve per box.

"Right," Elizabeth whispered. Her mind was spinning. Her heart was pumping. "Twelve per box."

So why are there only five left?

Two sheets of two and one separate one . . .

Elizabeth rattled the box. Something was wedged in the bottom of it. She looked inside.

A crumpled condom wrapper. Opened. Seal broken. Condom missing, presumed used.

Why . . . ?

Elizabeth stared hard and unblinking at the box. And in that moment her whole world shrank and collapsed into the single blue object before her eyes. She turned it over again. She looked at the label. She carefully checked the bright orange sale price tag.

In a sudden burst of motion Elizabeth stuffed the condoms back in, shut the box, and shoved it back down behind the bed. She wiped her hands down on the front of her jeans again and again. Her throat began to close up with horrible heart-thumping panic.

Tom and . . . Dana Upshaw?

Her mind flashed back. Images. Horrible, dark images. Tom's distracted, guilty face. Halting conversations. Awkward looks. Strange silences. Abrupt arguments.

"No," Elizabeth whispered. She closed her eyes. "No. No. *No.*"

"May I help you, sir?" the woman behind the hospital gift shop counter asked.

"No, thanks," Danny replied. He turned away from the paperback stand. He flipped through a rack of men's T-shirts. He studied the get-well flower arrangements in the shop's glass cooler.

"We have some very nice gift packages over here," the woman said.

"Thank you," Danny said, moving toward the glass wall that separated the gift shop from the hospital lobby. From where he was standing, he had a clear view of the reception area. All he had to do now was wait.

"Well, let me know if I can help you," the woman said.

"Uh-huh," Danny said. For a moment he stood and smiled back. Then he looked over and saw a large group passing by the reception area.

He watched carefully from behind the greeting card rack. Then, to his great relief, Mr. and Mrs. Ricci passed through. Still hidden, he watched as they walked tiredly through the lobby and out the automatic glass doors.

Danny had met Isabella's parents several times. But there was no way he could face them right now. How could he possibly explain to them how Isabella had slipped out of his protection? How could he look into their accusing eyes? How could he make them understand that he'd done everything he could to keep Isabella from hurting herself?

Finally Danny left the gift shop and headed for room 428. Danny grabbed the rail on the door, realizing that his back was wet with panicky sweat. He hadn't seen her since the morning after the accident.

When he pushed open the door and walked in, all he could see was Isabella's tiny, bruised face lying under a web of bandages, wires, and tubing. A monitor blinked and beeped steadily amid a tangle of wires and machines. Intravenous solution dripped into her left arm, which was now stained purple. A massive cast still encased her other arm, which lay helplessly at her side.

Danny felt his knees buckling. He drew up a chair and pulled it next to her. He took her slender hand in his.

"Isabella?" Danny said in a cracked whisper. "Izzy, can you hear me?"

He looked down at her fingers, tipped with raggedly broken nails, and stroked them, tears springing to his eyes. "Please wake up." Danny sniffed and took a deep breath. "Look. Maybe I shouldn't have come here. Maybe I should have kept all my anger away." He looked at her closed eyelids for any sign of movement. But there was none.

"Isabella?" he repeated. He shook her limp hand a little. "Izzy?"

Danny dropped her lifeless hand. He sat back and clenched his fists. "Why can't you open your eyes for just a *moment?*"

Isabella's face lay perfectly still, like stone.

Danny drew close. "I can't understand why you did this to yourself, Iz. You are so beautiful. So . . . perfect. How could you have . . . ?"

Danny buried his head in his arms, sobbing. "Why wouldn't you listen to me?"

For a long while Danny just sat there with his head in his hands, listening to the steady beep of the monitor and the whisper of Isabella's shallow breath. The air was thick with the smell of sickness. The smell cramped his muscles and suffocated him.

Tears began to flow, fast and furious. His life—it was in ruins. His future—destroyed. Everything he'd ever wanted was galloping away from him, faster and faster and faster.

"Excuse me," a low voice said behind him. "Visiting hours are over now."

Danny turned slowly around and saw Isabella's doctor standing in the doorway. "Oh."

He felt a hand on his shoulder. "I'm Dr. Gomez. We met right after the accident. Isabella's boyfriend, right?"

Danny nodded miserably. "Yeah."

"I just spoke to her parents," Dr. Gomez said quietly.

Danny looked over. "Wha-What did you tell them?"

Dr. Gomez paused. "We're very worried about Isabella's deteriorating neurological functions."

Danny froze.

"The subdural hematoma should have stabilized

233

by now," she said carefully. "She should have regained consciousness."

"What does that mean?" Danny demanded, standing up.

Dr. Gomez looked grave. "She's still breathing on her own, and that's good. But we're very concerned about coma—"

"Coma?"

"It's a possibility we must face," Dr. Gomez said firmly. "If she doesn't regain consciousness soon, an increasingly comatose state and perhaps serious brain damage are likely."

Danny stood up and turned to face her. "Well, what are you doing about it?"

Dr. Gomez looked at him calmly. "It's the kind of medical situation that requires time and patience."

"Well, I don't *have* any patience!"

"Right now the best course is to wait for—"

"I don't want to wait!" Danny said in a louder voice. He squeezed his fists tightly at his sides. His anger mounted so quickly and with such intensity, he had to make himself look shakily down at the ground instead of into the doctor's eyes.

"I'm so sorry," Dr. Gomez murmured, turning to leave.

"You're not sorry!" Danny shouted. "*I'm* sorry. *No one* is sorrier than I am. Don't you understand? *No one* is sorrier!"

"Nick!" Jessica screamed.

On the other side of the house she heard an

234

engine starting, followed by the screech of wheels tearing down the driveway and down the street.

Jessica scrambled out of the bushes. Then she ran around to the entrance at the other side of the house and ripped off her knit cap. Once she reached the door, she tore it open and ran inside. By the light of her small flashlight she could barely make out Nick's still body on the floor.

"Nick!" Jessica knelt down beside him, panicking. She touched him helplessly. "Please be OK. Nick . . . oh, you've got to open your eyes. Please."

Nick groaned softly. A red, ragged bruise ran along one cheek, and blood trickled from a cut on his temple. His feet stirred, and after another moment his eyelids began fluttering open.

Slowly he lifted his hand to his head. "Oh, man."

"Ohmigosh," Jessica cried. "I've got the cell phone. I'm calling an ambulance now."

"No." Nick took her wrist and gripped it so hard, she dropped the phone. "No."

"But you need a doctor!" Jessica insisted. Tears coursed down her face.

Slowly Nick sat up. His face was contorted with pain. "No, Jessica. I made . . . a mistake."

"You need help!"

Nick waved her away and tried to stand up. "I shouldn't have come. I shouldn't have . . . brought you."

"No, no, no . . ."

"No ambulance. I want . . . to keep . . . this quiet."

Jessica sobbed. She held his elbow and tried to help him up. Unable to stand, Nick dropped to the floor. Jessica fell alongside him.

Nick rubbed his head. "What happened?"

"He knocked you out with the butt of his gun," Jessica said through her tears. She sat up and stroked Nick's forehead. "He pointed his gun at you and started talking crazy. He took the tape, Nick. He sounded high, but—"

"He was definitely high," Nick said. He leaned his brawny shoulder into Jessica's side for support. "And now . . . he knows . . . I'm a cop."

"What if he comes back?" Jessica cried, her eye on the door.

Nick touched the wound on his temple. "He will . . . one way or another." He slumped harder against her until his head fell into her lap.

"Nick! Don't leave me!" Jessica wailed.

His eyes blinked heavily, then closed completely. "It doesn't . . . look . . . good, Jess," he whispered.

Will Nick Fox live long enough to put Clay behind bars—and save Jessica from his deadly plans? Find out in Sweet Valley University #43, **THE PRICE OF LOVE.**